# SANCTIFIED

Joseph Edwards earned his first university diploma in French Language and Civilization from the University of Lyon, France in 1965. He later did graduate studies in both Romance Languages and philosophy at The University of North Carolina – Chapel Hill. He earned a juris doctorate from the University of Toledo, Ohio and an LLM in international and comparative law from the University of Brussels, Belgium. He grew up in eastern North Carolina and now lives on a farm in middle Tennessee. He practices law and his practice is currently limited to federal criminal defense.

*Terian*

*All the best!*

*Joseph F. Edwards*

JOSEPH F. EDWARDS

# Sanctified

*Sanctified*
Published by Cara Press

Copyright © 2013 Joseph F. Edwards

Book design by Maureen Cutajar
www.gopublished.com

ISBN 978-0-9836530-0-4

*To my young'uns Manuel, Shayne, Megan, and Jill,*
*who all have stories in them*

# FOREWORD

You can skip Book Two of this novel and still get the story, but if you want the full literary load you must read the whole thing. I've spent more than fifty years working on Book Two. Enjoy!

# BOOK ONE
# THE MOUNTAIN

# MINNIE FLETCHER

The night of the first cross burning on Cherokee Ridge, well past midnight of a warm night in May, three men knocked on Minnie Fletcher's door to request her services. Miss Minnie got out of bed and put on a house robe and came to the door. Such late night calls were not unusual for Miss Minnie.

She lived in a house out at the edge of town where she grew her garden and kept a milk cow and some laying hens and raised a few pigs each year, like most people in these parts. But also like everybody on the mountain she needed at least some income, so she provided a most unusual service. Miss Minnie could talk the fire out of you.

Everybody on the mountain knew that if you got burned the most expedient and the cheapest way to get relief was to go to Miss Minnie. Her emergency room was wherever she chose to see you when you got there; sometimes it would be her porch, sometimes her living room, sometimes her kitchen, sometimes her garden. It didn't matter, and she took all comers. Miss Minnie always said there was no charge for her services because it was God that gave her the ability to "talk the far outcha", but almost everybody who came for help left a few coins on her porch or the kitchen table when they left. Those who didn't have any coins to leave would come back in a few days with a string of fish, or a rabbit they had just caught and dressed, or other produce of the mountain, including an occasional pint jar of a clear liquid that just about everybody around these parts appreciated, including Miss Minnie.

Miss Minnie's place was the only fully integrated institution on the mountain at the time. If a Negro was there first

and then a Cherokee and then a hifalutin White Man arrived, the order in which she performed her healing art was
Negro, Cherokee, hifalutin White Man. Everyone was fine
with that. Her place was neutral territory; those who came
to her place came for relief from pain. They did not come to
fight or to belittle anyone else who might be there, and so
she was able to provide her services to all who came, and she
never refused her services to anyone. She would even let
these people use the telephone that hung on the wall in her
living room next to the kitchen door. This was completely
out of the question for most white people on the mountain;
they would not allow Negroes or Cherokee to talk into their
telephone for fear of catching something.

If the burn was blistered real bad, or if the skin was gone
and you could see the quick, Miss Minnie would go ahead and
talk the pain out of you and smear some lard or butter on the
wound and then send you to the doctor so he could work on
you and try to keep you from getting infected. She couldn't do
anything about infection. Even the doctors in town recognized that her ministrations were as successful as theirs, and
perhaps even more successful, with burns that didn't destroy
the skin. The consensus in the medical community was that
somehow Miss Minnie had acquired the ability to hypnotize;
since she frequently sent bad burns to the hospital or to local
physicians, they respected her and accepted her as a healer.
They simply could not argue with her results. Unlike these
licensed professional healers, however, Miss Minnie owed no
duty of secrecy or confidentiality to anyone.

Miss Minnie flipped the porch light on and looked through
the screen at the three men standing at her front door.

"Howdy Miss Minnie. I'm Johnny Mitchell from over on
Mitchell's Ridge. This here's Milton and he just got his hand
burned purdy bad and he needs for ya to talk the far outn' it
if ya will. This here other fella's a friend o' ours from over in
Barlow County. Name's Lester."

She looked at their faces in the porch light; she didn't
know any of them. She opened the screen door. "Come on

in and take a seat here in the living room. I'll be back in a minute."

Miss Minnie went into her bedroom and shut the door; she took her chamber pot from under her bed and squatted on it. The men could hear her urinating. After a few moments she came back into the living room and motioned for Johnny to pull up a chair by hers and have Milton sit down.

"Hold your hand out here so I can see it."

She looked carefully. The burn covered his entire hand. Skin had already started peeling away from the quick. Milton was agitated but he was trying to control himself and not show his pain.

"This is pretty bad. What happened?"

"We wuz just having some fun over at one of the Cherokee farms and Milton spilled some gas on his hand when he wuz splashin' it on the cross, and then when he struck the match his hand and his sleeve caught far – just kinda flashed right up and then kept on burning. He was jumping around screaming still standing right next to the cross so several of us jumped on him and jerked him away so the rest of'im wouldn' catch on far."

Miss Minnie looked at Milton's face and attempted to look into his eyes but he looked away. She began passing her hand in a circular motion over his hand and chanting in a low voice. She finally was able to look Milton in the eye as she continued chanting for several minutes. Milton began to calm down and after awhile he appeared to be no longer in pain. Lester watched.

"Shore looks like he's better," Lester said to Johnny. "But I betcha he won't be strikin' the matches over at the Rogers place tomorrow night. That hand's a mess." He grinned and looked at Milton's hand and then at Miss Minnie. Two of his front teeth were missing, one on top and one on the bottom. He looked proudly at Johnny.

Johnny glared at him.

The Rogers place was a little farm over on Cherokee Ridge just outside of Cherokee Town, a grouping of habitations where some of the Cherokee people lived and had their gardens and backyard livestock. Some claimed that those Rogers were part of the same roots as the Will Rogers family out in Oklahoma but nobody ever bothered to trace it back. The Cherokee people on our mountain were descendants of those who had avoided the forced removal to the western Indian lands a hundred years before, either by hiding or by exemption because they lived on private lands instead of Indian lands. Their number had increased considerably since the Trail of Tears; they were now back up to about five percent of the total population. They were good hard-working folk that stayed out of trouble and took care of their own. Miss Minnie had talked the fire out of many of them over the years, and over the years some of their old people had taught her many of their herbal remedies.

"No, I don't believe he will either," Miss Minnie said as she stood. "Wait here a minute while I go mix'im up a lard salve to rub over it till he can go to the doctor. But before I do ya'll need to listen to me – he needs to go straight from here to the doctor 'cause that hand can get bad infected. We can go ahead and call the doctor now. Ya'll can use my phone."

"I'll letcha put the lard on, but I ain't gonna be goin' to no doctor," Milton said.

Miss Minnie glanced at Milton and with a nod and the faintest hint of a smile she stepped into her kitchen. She returned a few minutes later with a paper cup in her hand.

"I've fixed you up some burn salve here. Your hand won't hurt for another ten or fifteen minutes after you leave here. You need to let your hand be calming for another five minutes or so after you leave here and then take a blob of this here salve in your good hand and smear it all over your burned hand real quick so it won't hurt so bad while you're rubbing it on. If it's hurtin' too bad, get one of these here boys to rub it on for you. But it shouldn' be hurtin' yet at that point. And you be sure you go straight from here to the doctor. He'll give you something for your pain when you get there. You can get to the hospital from here easy in fifteen or twenty minutes."

"I'll rub it on myself and I ain't goin' to no doctor. My mama used to use butter. You sure this lard'll work?"

Miss Minnie handed him the paper cup containing the salve. "It'll work."

The men stood and Johnny laid four quarters on the table next to the lamp.

"I'm tellin' ya now young man, you're gonna need to see a doctor for that hand less'n you want to lose it."

Milton smirked, and the men got in their pickup truck and left.

Miss Minnie picked up the phone and called the hospital and told the shift nurse in the emergency room that a young man with a badly burned hand would be arriving in about forty-five minutes. The nurse asked her why it would take so long for them to get there being as how her place wasn't fifteen minutes from the hospital. Miss Minnie told her it was because they weren't going to be going there straight from her place, that they were heading out to Mitchell's Ridge first but after about twenty minutes of driving they would be turning around and heading back into town to go to the hospital. She said they would be driving a lot faster coming back into town so they should be arriving at the hospital in just about forty-five minutes.

———◆———

Johnny drove out of town and soon the men were on the narrow curving roads leading to Mitchell's Ridge and Johnny's place where the men were staying. They didn't speak. After about five minutes of hard driving and a few miles down the road, Johnny pulled over and stopped.

"You want me to rub that salve on ya?"

"Naw, I'll do it. Here, hold this cup."

Milton took a blob of the salve about the size of an egg in his left hand and quickly rubbed it all over his burned hand, and thoroughly between his fingers. It didn't hurt.

"She shore nuff knew what she was doing ditn she?" said Lester. "That's the first time I seen anybody talk the far outta somebody."

When Milton had thoroughly coated his hand with Miss Minnie's salve, Johnny pulled back onto the road and drove on toward his place. Within a few minutes Milton started breathing in deeply and exhaling deeply and making grunting and moaning noises that the others could hear over the sounds of the truck. A few moments later he began to flail around in the pickup. He was sitting in the middle between Johnny and Lester and suddenly he leaned over in front of Lester to hold his hand out the window in the wind. After another minute or so he began to yell. Johnny asked him if he wanted to go back to Miss Minnie's for some more talking and Milton said he never wanted to go there again, that she hadn't done him any good at all except for just a few minutes and that now he was hurtin' worse than when he went to her house and that in fact he was hurtin' worse than he had ever hurt in his life.

Johnny drove on and after two or three minutes Milton had completely lost his composure – he was jumping around wildly inside the cab, constantly yelling. He crawled onto Lester's lap to get his hand farther out into the wind and stayed there until Lester finally managed to get out from under him and move to the middle next to Johnny. None of the men had ever experienced this much activity in the cab of a pickup truck, and by now Johnny's main concern was to keep from running off the road and wrecking the truck.

Suddenly Milton yelled that he needed to see a doctor. Johnny yelled back that they were a good twenty to thirty minutes from the nearest doctor, which would be the emergency room doctor, and that he might not even be there at this time of night but might have to be waked up and called in, and besides, he had just said that he watn' gonna go see no doctor. Milton yelled back that under the circumstances he had changed his mind and that now he did want to see a doctor and that he didn't care what the doctor was doing he needed to see'im right now.

That settled it. Johnny slowed and did a U-turn and sped back toward the hospital in town. Milton kept his hand out in the wind and yelled and bounced all the way to the hospital. When they pulled up to the emergency room the duty nurse was dozing at her desk but Milton's screams woke her. She took a quick look at Milton's greasy hand and said, "I'm going to have to call the doctor. It'll be about twenty minutes before he can get here."

"Jesus God Almighty woman! I cain't wait no twenty minutes. Why the hell don't ya'll keep a doctor here all the time? Don't you know a man might need to come see a doctor any time of the day or night?" He was still screaming.

The nurse looked at his hand again and appeared to be a little woozy herself. "There's a colored doctor already here in the hospital over on their side, but you probably don't want to go over there do you?"

Milton yelled back that he just needed to see a doctor that it didn't matter what part of the hospital he was in that what mattered was his pain and that he needed to do something right now not in twenty minutes. He was jumping around and holding his right wrist with his left hand and bending forward as if bowing and then standing back up and then bending his knees and grimacing and then straightening up, as he screamed and yelled. Down the hall a couple of heads popped out of their rooms and stared toward the emergency area.

"He looks like he's really hurting," the nurse said to Johnny and Lester.

"Yes Ma'am, it shore seems so. It wuz all I could do to drive'im here with him a jumpin' around inside the truck and makin' such a fuss the whole way."

The nurse managed to get Milton into a wheel chair and rolled him through the dividing doors and into the colored section of the hospital emergency department with Milton yelling and kicking his legs as she pushed him down the hall.

Milton was still hollering when Dr. Allison helped the nurse put him on an examining table and looked closely at Milton's hand. He spoke to the nurse and a few seconds later she handed Dr. Allison a syringe. He found a vein and gave him the injection and within a few moments Milton was sedated. The doctor examined the dark brown salve that thickly coated his patient's burned hand. He lifted the hand and leaned forward and smelled the salve and then asked the nurse to bring the other two men in and when they arrived he asked them what had happened.

"Milton burned his hand." Johnny left out the part about the cross burning.

"I'd say it sure looks like he burned his hand."

The doctor knew that he wasn't going to get any more useful information about the burn from these boys.

"We taken'im over to Miss Minnie's to get the far talked out'n it and she did it and it worked. But she told'im he needed to see a doctor right away 'cause of the infection, and he said he watn' gonna go see no doctor. She mixed'im up a salve and told'im to wait a few minutes 'fore puttin' it on and he did it just the way she said. We'uz two or three miles down the road 'fore Milton rubbed the salve on his burned hand real good. But it watn' long after he smeared on the salve that he started yelling and screaming and beatin' around inside the truck and stickin' his hand out the window, and then he decided to come to the hospital."

Dr. Allison thanked Johnny and Lester and sent them back over to the white side and picked up the phone and called Miss Minnie.

"Miss Minnie, this is Dr. Allison. Sorry to have to call you at three o'clock in the morning."

"That's okay. I've been waitin' up for a call from y'all."

"Miss Minnie, there's a man here with a burned hand, and the men with him say that you talked the fire out of him a little while ago."

"Yes I did Dr. Allison. It worked real good, and I told him that he was still gonna need to see a doctor right now because it was a real bad burn. I could already see the quick all over his hand and between his fingers. But he said he wasn't gonna go see no doctor, so I mixed him up a little burn salve in some lard that would cover his burned hand real good and kill the germs."

"Yes I saw the coating on his hand, and what did you put in the salve Miss Minnie?"

"Well, just things that I knew would kill the germs, like salt and snuff and cayenne pepper powder."

"Yes, I thought it was something like that. I thought I smelled the snuff."

"Yes Sir. They mentioned something about a burning at the Rogers place tomorrow night, Dr. Allison, and I just felt like this hand really needed to be treated before they did something like that."

He paused, sensing that she was telling him something.

"Yes Miss Minnie. And how much of this salt and snuff and cayenne pepper powder did you use?"

"Well, I used about a cup of lard, didn't put any butter in it – butter's been kinda scarce here lately since my cow dried up – and I put a heaping tablespoon each of the salt and snuff and cayenne pepper powder. Then I mixed it all together real good, and then I mixed in a little bit of Pinee so it would smell like a salve ought to. And they say the Pinee'll kill germs too and keep flies off to boot. Don't you think that was about right Dr. Allison?"

*He hadn't seen this particular formulation in his materia medica classes at Harvard Medical School but he would certainly have to agree with her science. She knew without a doubt that the application of this salve would get this man to the hospital and would prompt a call to her from the attending physician. These mountain people often amazed him. What would have happened if he had not been the doctor on duty this night? Surely most of the doctors would do precisely what he was going to do; but if not, certainly Miss Minnie would have taken the next step and notified someone who would know what to do. Obviously her objective was to communicate the*

*information about the plans for the Rogers place without com-*
*promising her neutrality, but he was satisfied that she would*
*have done whatever was necessary to get the message out.*

Like most doctors on the mountain he moonlighted in the emergency department for a few shifts each month, and he saw some strange things; but this thing with Miss Minnie was a first for him.

"Yes Miss Minnie, I think that was just about right. Yes Ma'am. Well, we always appreciate you, Miss Minnie. If you ever need anything you let me know. You get yourself some rest now, and thank you. I'll take care of it from here."

He cradled the telephone and walked back to his patient and checked his pulse. He would keep him sedated for a few hours – at least until the doctor for the next shift arrived. He would get a nurse in here to clean the salve off the patient's hand while he was sedated. The other boys could wait on the white side. He would get a message to them later in the morning. Now he needed to get a message to the Rogers family, and he was pretty sure they didn't have a telephone. The day shift doctor who would relieve him would be arriving shortly. He sensed that big trouble lay ahead.

# JOHNNY WOLF

**D**r. Allison left the hospital at six o'clock when the doctor taking the next shift arrived. He stopped by his house and told his wife he would be late for breakfast, then drove to his preacher's house. The preacher was up and cooking breakfast; he poured Dr. Allison a cup of coffee. The doctor told the preacher what had happened in the emergency room and what Miss Minnie had said about the Rogers place and the burning that was to take place there that evening. He finished his coffee and declined the preacher's offer of breakfast, and upon the preacher's assurance that he would get the message to the Cherokee as soon as he finished eating, Dr. Allison drove home and had another cup of coffee and breakfast with his wife.

As soon as he finished eating, the preacher drove out to Cherokee Ridge and found Johnny Wolf. It was already a hot morning late in May. School would be out for the summer in less than two weeks. But for now the preacher knew that Johnny would be leaving for school in a few minutes. This was the second message that the preacher had received this morning. A man came over from Free Town – the Colored section of town, known by many as Nigger Town, at the edge of which the preacher lived – and told him that word was getting around that the Klan was bragging about how they were going to burn down a Cherokee house somewhere tonight, but nobody knew which one. Now he had the connection.

"There's gonna be trouble tonight Johnny. Just wanted to let you know."

"What's happening Preacher?"

"Word's out that some of the Klan are gonna burn the Rogers place tonight, not just a cross."

Johnny looked out over the valley below Cherokee Town. For some time now he had felt that something like this was coming. For months the Klan had been making noises about the Cherokee. They had even slashed some Cherokee tires and had shot two of their dogs. He could feel the evil coming.

"Thank ya Preacher. We'll take care of it. Looks like the time's come. Lord willin' we'll return the favor to you and your folks soon." The old black man looked at him and made a little nod but said nothing. Johnny watched him walk to his car. He loved these people almost as much as he loved his Cherokee people.

Johnny was a man of small stature in his early forties who was generally recognized as the leader of the Cherokee people on the mountain. He had graduated from the white high school and had gone down to Chapel Hill and worked his way through a four year degree in seven years, sweeping the floors of Old East and flipping burgers in the cafeteria and various cafes and restaurants around town. He finally got a white jacket job at the Carolina Inn where he worked until he graduated, building up his cash reserves from the generous tips he received from affluent diners. He came back to the mountain with more money than he had taken with him seven years earlier. He took over the coaching job at the Negro high school and taught social studies there. Johnny was one of those rare souls who wanted to earn just enough to meet his basic needs and nothing more. He had foresworn the pursuit of money beyond his basic needs to pursue his mission, and this empowered him in the sense that he was free from many of the burdens and constraints imposed upon someone who was driven by money.

Johnny took a great interest in the sociology of the mountain. The segregation had always disgusted him, and he had determined that no man would diminish his humanity because he was not a Caucasian. Before he left Chapel Hill to return to the mountain he had already made a commitment to resist racist assaults against his people and the Negroes using whatever means might be necessary. He had decided that no matter what happened because of his race when he returned to the mountain, or how painful it might be, he would never back down. If he had to spill his own blood to have the freedom that he envisaged for his people and the coloreds so be it.

The preacher's news made him angry. For years he had wondered what it was about these people that made it possible for them to harm other people because of the color of their skin. No matter how you viewed it, no matter that this mountain was mostly populated with good people, there was here – as there was just about everywhere – a spirit of evil that existed side by side with the good. It was a spirit that wormed its way into a man and took him over and made him less than what humans are supposed to be, and it drove him to do things that destroyed innocent people's lives. It hadn't been ten years ago that the Klan had lynched a twelve year old Negro boy right outside of town. They claimed he had whistled at a fifteen year old white girl. For decades they had burned down houses and shot dogs and livestock that belonged to Negroes, and neither this sheriff nor the one before him nor the one before that one ever did anything about it. They never did *anything* about it! They would tell the Negro man or the Cherokee man to let the law take its course. Fools! How can an intelligent man tell them this when the law never did anything for them when they were the victims? What law? He knew as most real men know that there comes a time in a man's life when he just has to take a stand and take action, and let the consequences be what they will. Sometimes the law just doesn't work. That's when a man has to appeal to a higher law, and Johnny knew what he was going to do. Two hundred years was long enough. The time had come.

Johnny thought about what the Klan apparently had
planned for tonight. But whoever had made the decision for
the Klan to come to the Rogers place tonight had made a
major mistake. There was not a Cherokee on the whole
mountain who had the slightest fear of these Klan imbeciles.
He could not fathom why they would risk assaulting his
people, other than that they were quite simply stupid. The
truth was, they were not the mountain rabble; they were
mostly average people – farmers, mechanics, day laborers
who considered themselves better than others because they
were Caucasians. That was certainly their call, but one thing
was for sure: there would be unhappy white women on the
mountain in the morning. The Klan might be able to use fear
and intimidation to control people in some places, but it
wasn't going to happen here on Cherokee Ridge.

Johnny finished his coffee and got in his pickup and
drove out toward the Rogers house. He had an hour and a
half before he had to be at school. He stopped at several
houses along the way and told the men to meet him at the
Rogers farm at noon to discuss a community emergency.
Knowing their attitude toward the clock – the people
around here called it Indian time – he asked them to be
there right at noon because he was on the government clock.
This would give them time to finish their morning tasks, and
since he didn't have cafeteria duty this week he could leave
school for an hour or so to meet with the men. They told
him they would be there at noon.

The Klan had started disputing with the Cherokee people several months back, saying that white folk were racially
superior to the Cherokees and that the Indians didn't have
any business being around the white folks just like the niggers didn't. And the Cherokees said that's fine. This aggra-
vated some of the Klan members so the Klan said they would
deal with the Indians just like they dealt with the niggers,

and they picked out a family of Cherokees and put on their white robes and hoods and went over to that family's house one night and put a cross in the yard and started burning it. The problem for the Klan was that this midnight burning didn't scare the Cherokee. So the Klan put out word they were going to do some burning at somebody else's house the next night and they didn't intend to limit it to a cross this time. This didn't scare the Cherokee either.

It would not have been the first time that the Klan had burned down a house on the mountain. In fact over the years they had torched several houses and barns and other structures, including a church or two, that belonged to black folk. Johnny made a decision this morning that the Klan had committed its last burning on this mountain.

———————

There was a crowd of Cherokee men at the Rogers house just after noon. Johnny guessed eighteen or twenty at first glance. He told the men what the preacher had told him earlier.

"I'm going to send the Rogers women to somebody else's house right after supper this evening, and I'm comin' up here with my 22 rifle and my 30-30 and two or three boxes of ammo for each one of 'em. I'm gonna wait for these imbeciles. When they get here and light the fire the first thing I'm gonna do is shoot as many of 'em in the legs as I can, and then I'm gonna shoot the lights out of their vehicles and I'm gonna shoot their tires, and when I've done that I'm gonna start shooting their windshields and their radiators and any other parts of them trucks that I can hit from where I'm shooting. I'm not going to try to kill anybody, but I'm gonna put a hurtin' on 'em.

"Any of y'all that want to can join me. I think we need to put a stop to this nonsense before it gets started. How many of you think you can be here tonight?"

Every man there said he would be back by dark with a rifle and plenty of ammo.

"Alright. About half of you bring 22's for shooting their legs and the rest of you bring your huntin' rifles for shootin' the vehicles. I've got to get on to the schoolhouse so y'all work that out before you leave.

"When you get here take that tractor path past the house and park in that little field back behind those woods and come on back up to the house. We'll wait behind the bushes till we see'em comin'. Everybody bring some short pieces of rope for tourniquets. We'll probably need'em."

———————

The night of the second and last cross burning on Cherokee Ridge, around midnight, the men who had gathered at the Rogers house saw the headlights of the Klan cars and pickups snaking up the curves of the farm road to the house. The Cherokee had taken positions where the Klansmen couldn't see them when their headlights shone on the house. The Klansmen jumped out of their vehicles and set up the cross in the Rogers' front yard and set it afire, and once the cross was in full blaze a white robe ran up to the cross and lit a torch with it and threw the burning torch onto the front porch. One of the Cherokee men jumped onto the porch, grabbed the torch and threw it back into the crowd of white robes.

"Now!" Johnny yelled, and the Cherokees who had the 22 caliber rifles started shooting the Klansmen in the legs, aiming about knee high; and the ones with the high powered rifles shot at all the cars and pickups. They shot out the lights and tires of every Klan car and pickup there except for one or two at the rear of the group of vehicles which managed to turn around quickly and drive away and even they had bullet holes in them. For two or three minutes the sound of the gunfire was like the finale of the fireworks at the annual county fair.

White robes scattered everywhere and men were screaming. The Cherokees stopped shooting and let all the men that still had functioning legs run into the woods and make their way back to wherever they came from. The Cherokee men went out and checked on the men that were lying on the ground or crawling around in the yard. They pulled the hoods off all of them. They knew most of them. One of the men lying in the yard moaning was a deputy sheriff that everybody on the mountain knew. Both his legs were a mangled mess from the knees down, shot all to pieces; and he had a small caliber rifle wound in each hand that he had received when he had instinctively tried to block the rifle fire with his hands. And to top it off one of the pickups that had managed to leave had run right over his legs as he lay moaning in the driveway.

There were seventeen disabled vehicles, every one of which had shotguns or rifles, or both, and several boxes of ammunition in it. Everybody on the mountain that had a vehicle drove around with a gun in it – that was normal here – but these Klansmen were known for carrying around a lot more firepower than other folk.

"Get their guns and ammo." Johnny walked among the injured, looking at each man's face.

The other men checked each Klansman for injuries. Several of the men gathered the guns and ammo from the Klan vehicles and piled them in the Rogers' pickup truck while others applied tourniquets.

"Whatcha got?" Johnny asked.

"Looks like fifty-seven long guns and a hundred and twenty somethin' boxes of ammo – I ain't counted the pistols yet, but there's a pile of 'em – I'd say about thirty," said the man who was stacking the guns and ammo. "Where we gonna take 'em?"

"Nigger Town."

"Jesus!" moaned a bleeding Klansman.

Johnny looked at him and smiled. "Sweetheart, you'da been better off calling on Jesus before comin' out here tonight. I betcha anything he'd a tried to tell ya not to commit this foolishness."

"We're gonna divide'em up 'bout equal for all the colored churches over there in town and let the preachers give'em out." Johnny spoke loud enough for the moaning men to hear him. "I'm sure you ladies'd be welcome to attend some of their services and ask for your guns back. They probly won't even make you sit on the back row. That'd be my guess. I don't think they'll give ya your guns back though. I imagine most of you girls are familiar with the ancient maxim 'To the victor go the spoils' and as you can see we're the victor here tonight so these guns and ammo belong to us now; they're our spoils and we can give them to anybody we please. And it will please us to know that your colored neighbors have in their possession a reasonable amount of guns and ammo for the foreseeable future. Course y'all can file a complaint with the sheriff if ya want to. But one thing's for sure – we don't plan to have any more cross burnings on this mountain. You think y'all could agree?" Johnny asked sweetly.

Most of the wounded men just continued to moan, and bleed. The Cherokee men moved about the men, examining them and tightening tourniquets as needed.

After they had done what they considered necessary to prevent any deaths, all of them, including the male members of the Rogers family, got into their vehicles and left. Somebody in the bunch stopped at one of the Cherokee houses on the ridge that had a telephone and called the sheriff's office and told them what had happened and to go get the people that had been shot and told them to have the vehicles moved off the Cherokee farm by sundown the next day because they were all coming back to the Rogers place at dark and would totally destroy any vehicle that was still there.

Within a couple of hours the Rescue Squad's two ambulances had delivered fifteen men with shot up legs to the emergency room that was designed to handle no more than three people at a time. Some of the men had to be put over in the Negro part of the hospital and a colored doctor worked on them. By the time they had all been treated and admitted, everybody on the mountain knew what had happened. The next day many businesses were closed and many farms unplowed. There were even two substitute teachers called in at the white high school. The school records reflected that the two regular teachers had been accidentally wounded in the legs while coon hunting the night before.

The Cherokee family returned home the night after the second cross burning with a crowd of friends and resumed their normal routine. The Cherokees on the mountain never had any further trouble from the Klan, and the sheriff never brought any charges against the Indians, who couldn't have cared less, or the Klansmen, but he did fire the deputy who had been shot up. The colored doctor had had to amputate both his legs about six inches below the knees to save his life, so he couldn't have worked as a deputy anyway. That deputy swore that he would still have his legs if a white doctor had worked on him. Daddy said that he would still have his legs if he hadn't gone out to that Cherokee farm wearing a white robe and a hood.

As it turned out, many of those who had been able to flee had been shot and had small caliber bullet wounds in their legs. They trickled into the emergency room and various doctors' offices over the next few days as infections set in and their home remedies failed. For the next week two or three Cherokee men hung out at the entrance to the emergency room and near the entrance to each of the various doctors' offices in town, and smiled encouragingly when one of the injured men hobbled in or was carried in by his family. In most cases they knew the injured men, and wrote their names down in a notebook as they entered the doctor's office or the emergency room. At the end of the week they turned all these names over to Johnny Wolf, who enlisted the assistance of some Cherokee high school girls to write, in the name of the Cherokee community, a get well card to each of the injured men and his family, including the two teachers who had gone coon hunting.

The towing company had worked all the next day following the second cross burning on Cherokee Ridge moving the

seventeen vehicles off the Cherokee farm. The sheriff had told
the towing company that every one of the vehicles better be
gone by sundown. The two body shops in town stayed busy
for the next three weeks plugging holes and replacing radiators and headlights and windshields. One of the shops was
slowed down considerably because one of its men was in the
hospital with a crushed knee cap and other leg injuries that he
sustained while he too was coon hunting. By the end of the
three weeks most of the medical staff on the mountain concluded that there must have been an influx of coons this spring
the likes of which this mountain had never experienced.
When one innocent medical novice indelicately questioned
the reported cause of the injury of one of his patients, noting
that one usually shoots upward into trees when coon hunting
at night, not toward the ground where legs usually reside, several of the mountain sages suggested that there must be a new
species of ground-hugging coon that had been brought in
from out west where there weren't any trees and thus the
coons didn't know how to climb them.

It would be difficult to describe accurately the hilarity of
the Cherokee when this explanation appeared in the Saturday edition of the newspaper. Although the Cherokee are
not often celebratory by nature, when this explanation was
offered in the newspaper they were moved to declare a
barbeque of four full grown pigs, which they gleefully denot-
ed as ground coons, and to this barbeque on the courthouse
square, or more accurately *in* the courthouse square because
they dug a long barbeque pit for the cooking, they invited
the whole Cherokee community, all of whom came, and all
the black preachers and Miss Minnie and the sheriff, who
also came. When someone pointed out that these pigs bore
only the slightest resemblance to coons, for example they
had four legs, a head, and a tail, the Cherokee solemnly noted that they were indeed like this new race of coons in two
important respects: the pigs, like these new ground coons,
could not climb trees; and when you shot them to dress
them out for human consumption, you shot them in the

head right between the eyes which is at about the same level as a human knee no matter how big the pig; this required that a man standing upright shoot downward as in the shooting of this new species of coon. The mountain seemed satisfied with this explanation.

The Cherokee drafted a special invitation to the barbeque for the men and their families whose names had been noted at the entrances to the emergency room and the various medical offices within the days following the incident at the Rogers house; none of the men came, but most of their women came and were warmly received by the Cherokee. The deputy whose legs had been amputated didn't have a woman, so following the barbeque and festivities on the courthouse lawn one of the Cherokee women packed up a meal and took it to him. When she brought the meal to him he got mad. She ignored his anger as she unpacked the meal. Then he started bawling. She put her hand on his shoulder and calmed him. Because both his hands were still heavily bandaged she started feeding him the barbeque and the slaw and the hush puppies, and finally he settled down and finished the meal. The next day she brought him another meal, and this continued daily for several months. He got some artificial limbs and she helped him learn to walk on them. A week before Christmas she took him home with her and married him in front of most of the people from Cherokee Ridge and a good number of people from Free Town. The Cherokee bride had cleaned the judge's house and the courthouse for several years and she got the judge to agree to come out to perform the legal ceremony, which occurred following the real ceremony which consisted of the little woman standing up and yelling out to the whole crowd "This here's my husband and I'm his wife from here on out! Anybody got a problem with that come see me about it and we'll git it straightened out right then and there." That settled it – nobody had any problems, and as soon as they had made their vows with the judge, everyone gathered near a cooking pit in the ground from which two pigs had been removed. They all, including the judge, ate the pigs and celebrated the marriage. Out of deference to the sensibilities of the groom no one said anything about ground coons.

About a month after the little Cherokee woman married the ex-deputy, she took him to a church in Free Town. As was the custom, she and her new husband sat at the back of the church since he was a white man. She had told the preacher about a week earlier that she was going to be there with her husband. The preacher preached about forgiveness and the love that God has for us and how Jesus wants us all to forgive each other and love each other no matter what we have done to each other in the past. At the end of the sermon the preacher made an alter call, inviting anyone to come forward if he had anything on his heart that he wished to share with the congregation. The deputy looked around for a moment and then took a step forward and then another, and by the time he got past the third or fourth row from the back, black hands at the end of each pew reached out to steady him as he anxiously moved forward on his new artificial feet. His woman walked behind him. When he reached the front he turned to the audience and looked down at the floor and simply said "I'm sorry," and he started sobbing, and his shoulders moved up and down and he kept sobbing. The singing had stopped and tears were coursing down black faces and the room was quiet except for the sobbing and the deputy kept crying as some of the men helped him stand there since he didn't have any toes to balance himself, and the Spirit of God filled the room and there was peace and healing on the mountain.

———◆———

Meanwhile, long before the union of the little Cherokee woman and the legless ex-deputy sheriff, the high sheriff himself spoke several times in the weeks following the big barbeque in town about what a great pig picking that was, and how it contributed to a sense of community on the mountain, especially since they had held it right down town on the courthouse square.

For most of the summer following the courthouse barbeque there was a general sense of peace on the mountain, except in the homes of the men who had been shot. The men who had been injured in the coon hunting accidents spent the ensuing weeks and months learning to walk again. Their wives did the work that their men would have been doing had they not been so unfortunately shot in the legs. The women punished their men for this by doing absolutely nothing for them. When the women cooked they prepared only enough for themselves. They couldn't skip milking the cows because the cows would die from mastitis, so they milked them, set aside enough for themselves to drink and to make just enough butter and clabber for their own consumption, and fed the rest to the pigs. The men had no milk to drink, no clabber to mix with cornbread, and no cornbread or biscuits unless they made it themselves. When they dressed their husbands' wounds the women would press and poke and scrub in such a way that the men yelled and broke out into sweats, and the women broke out into smiles. Then they went into the fields, where their husbands should have been, and did their own sweating, while anticipating with pleasure the changing of the men's dressings in the evening. In the evening the wounds were salted as was the custom then, to kill the germs, and the women would push the salt into the hole with a finger that was slightly larger than the hole to make sure it got deep enough to do some good. The men yelled, but they used all their strength to keep from yelling loud enough for their neighbors to hear them. These women generally had a very happy and productive summer.

Thus it was that over a year later, after what came to be known as The Trial, as if only one trial in all the history of the mountain had so distinguished itself from all the rest that it alone merited, indeed required, the use of the definite article without more, *The* Trial, and after what the judge did the day following the trial, Free Town (or as it was known to the sheriff, the Klansmen, and many others, Nigger Town) was probably the most well-armed concentration of colored people its size south of the Mason-Dixon line, or come to think of it, probably north of the Mason-Dixon line. Free Town was full of guns and ammunition and mad black folks. And all the inhabitants of Free Town considered that this was righteous because almost all the guns and ammunition had been distributed by congregations of the church in Free Town. This concentration of guns and ammunition among the coloreds would later become a source of great consternation among many on the mountain following The Trial.

# THE JUDGE

The judge who presided at The Trial was my father, Judge Jonathan Wesley Steadings. And although he was our judge, by definition a man of fairly high standing in our part of the country, he took life day by day and had his ups and downs like everyone on the mountain. Some people even said you couldn't tell he was a judge when he was off the bench because he might get in a scrap just like the next man and he hung around with some of the low lifes on the mountain. In other words although his status was hifalutin, hardly anyone on the mountain considered him to be hifalutin.

One day late in the summer following the Cherokee education of the Klan, a few weeks before our local music competition, Daddy and I were outside doing some yard work and Lady, our Bassett Hound, was hanging out with us, as dogs do. Mr. Higginbotham lived three houses down the street and he had some visitors from California who had brought a big dog with them. While we were doing the yard work, their dog came running down the street toward us and when he got to Lady he jumped on her and bit her on the neck. She yelped and started bleeding and went down but the dog kept biting her. Daddy picked up a shovel and hit the dog on the head with it, hard. It looked to me like the dog was knocked out, but in a moment he yelped and got up and when Daddy started at him again he ran back up toward Mr. Higginbotham's house with his tail between his legs yelping all the way. The California guy who owned the dog was standing outside and could see the attack from down the street, and when Daddy hit his dog the man came running down the street and rushed up to Daddy and started yelling right in his face.

Daddy just stood there looking at the man straight in the face and waited for him to finish yelling. The man stopped and stood menacingly in front of Daddy, and then Daddy said to him,

"Mister, I don't know you – never seen you before in my life, and I'm not going to say this but one time. My dog was down here in her own yard minding her own business, not bothering anybody, and your dog came running down here and picked a fight with my dog. So I took this shovel and I hit your dog in the head with it real hard." He motioned with the shovel toward the man, as if to make sure the man saw what he was talking about.

The man was getting madder.

Daddy paused for a moment.

"And now here *I* am down here in *my* own yard minding *my* own business not bothering anybody, and now *you* come running down here wanting to pick a fight with *me*."

Daddy still had the shovel in his hand.

And that's all he said. He didn't say "I'm the local judge" or "Get off my property" or anything like that. I could see the man was startled – this was not what he had expected. I could sense him processing the moment, perceiving the parallels, still wild eyed. He looked at the shovel in Daddy's hand for a moment and then turned around and stomped off. We never saw their dog again, and the next day the visitors were gone from the Higginbotham house before we ate breakfast. A few months later the Higginbothams moved out to California and we never heard from them again. But before they moved they would say hello and act like nothing had ever happened. Later that year Lady got hit by a car and died. Daddy cried when Mama told him what happened. Daddy pulled my wagon over to where Mama had drug Lady and picked her up and put her on the wagon, and he took that same shovel and buried her at the back of our vegetable garden. My granddaughter plays with that same wagon to this day, and I still have that shovel, and it's as good as it was fifty years ago, for gardening or whatever else.

———◆———

During the early evening of the night that Mama and Daddy worked until midnight moving me and J.C. to a downstairs bedroom, which was a few days after Mr. Higginbotham's California guest narrowly avoided getting knocked in the head with a shovel, we had the preacher and his wife and an older couple from church for supper.

As usual, everybody got there about an hour ahead of mealtime.

"Y'all come on in and sit a spell," Mama said, "I'll have you some ice tea out here in just a minute." Everyone went to the living room and started shootin' the breeze. This was story time, and it played out in living rooms and kitchens and around campfires all over the mountain about this time of day. This was the way news traveled from one side of the mountain to the other within hours. Most of the stories were about current events, or more particularly about what had happened to this person or that person recently. This included farms lost through foreclosure; farms sold, farms bought; births, deaths, illnesses, and other particularized troubles or victories of interest to all. Inevitably these conversations gradually became historical rather than current, reaching back into the past and tying it to the present, telling of the culture of the mountain and indeed contributing to it. This was a live, raw history of us – The Story, without which this mountain would not be *this* mountain.

And so the old man visiting us that evening told a couple of mountain stories, ones that we had all heard before but which we enjoyed every time we heard them. Many of these mountain tales were grounded in humor because we had to have it; we could not do without laughter in our lives and remain well, and so they had to be true, or mostly so, because we had to believe them if we were really to laugh, and then they were medicine for our community spirit. We rejoiced in the victories of our heroes, were gratified by the defeats of those on whom our disapproval rested and for some reason we laughed at the misfortunes and pain of those on whom we felt Justice, whether poetic or institutional, should be visited. But it seemed that our greatest delights and satisfaction ensued when we heard about or watched poetic justice in action.

This evening Daddy was in a particularly jovial mood, and when that was the case he often told a railroad story or two.

When he was in his early twenties Daddy left the mountain and worked for the railroad during the summer to earn money for college. He primarily did grunt work in the freight yards in Rocky Mount and Richmond, and he often traveled from one city to the other in a caboose.

Daddy was committed to our system of justice, but from my earliest memories I can recall him saying that justice does not reside solely in a courtroom. When he wanted to make the point that it is in the nature of human existence that we are often blessed with and should always welcome this poetic justice, Daddy delighted in telling about something that happened on one of these trips in the caboose. I heard the story many times and it was always the same in its essentials.

Daddy had been working in the yards in Rocky Mount and he was riding in the caboose of a short freight train up to Richmond where he was supposed to work in the yards up there for a few days. Two other men and the conductor were also in the caboose. The conductor was a big hairy man who made it a point to go to church wherever he was laid over for a day or two, if that was on a Wednesday night or a Sunday, but in his day-to-day activities he tended to order his subordinates around to serve his personal needs. Generally he did nothing for himself that he could get someone else to do for him.

This train moved along fairly fast on long straight stretches in rural areas, but it would slow down in more populated areas and stretches where the tracks had tight curves. There was a coal-burning stove in the caboose on which the men made their coffee and cooked their stew or whatever they were eating that day. And although the weather was hot and humid outside, the men could keep the caboose fairly cool in the summertime by opening its windows.

On this trip they were making a pot of coffee in a heavy enameled steel pot and it had just finished percolating to a rich, dark, bubbling brew. The train was going slow. There was one small booth in the caboose where the men ate two at a time, and the conductor was sitting in it facing the rear of the train; another man was sitting on the other side of the table in the booth facing the conductor. The booth was just one seat wide and was rather compact. It was a hot day but people drank coffee all day long back then. Daddy used to say a cup of hot coffee would cool you down in the summertime. All the men were dressed in their railroad overalls, and because of the heat the conductor wasn't even wearing a shirt.

"Git up and git me a cup of coffee," the conductor said to the man facing him.

The man got up and set a mug in front of the conductor and took the pot of still boiling coffee from the stove and started pouring coffee into the conductor's mug. Just as the man began pouring the coffee the engineer suddenly slammed on the train's brakes and instantly the stream of boiling coffee moved forward from the mug into the conductor's lap and up his chest to his neck and then down inside his overalls on his bare shirtless skin.

Daddy said the conductor just as instantly lost his composure. He tried to back away from the stream of boiling coffee but there was nowhere to go because the back of the booth stopped him, so he flailed and slapped at the coffee pot and its boiling stream which caused it to spill its full measure – the whole pot of coffee – onto his chest inside his overalls. The man who was pouring the coffee lost his balance and dropped the pot into the conductor's lap. Daddy said the conductor came out the side of the booth hollering and yelling and flailing and slapping and jumping, still trying to get the scalding liquid and the searing steel pot off his front side.

At this point in the story Daddy would often digress and talk about how we all, the simplest or even the most sophisticated of us, maintain a certain public composure, and that no matter how lowly or how hifalutin or powerful a person is there is a breakpoint at which composure no longer matters. When this breakpoint is reached it is not so much that one makes a decision to abandon one's composure but rather that one enters an ontological zone where composure doesn't matter for the simple reason that there is no issue of human relations there, and thus there is no social compact requiring a certain comportment by anyone in that zone. Daddy emphasized that when one enters that zone one is in a state of existence where there are no social constraints.

The digression often included a story about an event that occurred in one of the big law firms in Knoxville where Daddy was interviewing for a job right after he completed law school. All the candidates for the position had gone through the initial interviews and were finally being interviewed by the senior partner, who had recently completed two terms as a United States Senator before returning to his old law firm in Knoxville.

The senator was receiving two young lawyers at a time and Daddy was paired with the only female in the group of candidates. Daddy said she was a knockout gorgeous young woman, always adding that she was almost as pretty as Mama. Daddy and the young lady were escorted into the senator's office and he motioned to Daddy and the young lady to have a seat in a couple of straight back chairs across from him at a small coffee table where he was seated in a nice straight back captain's chair. He had beverages brought in and Daddy and the young lady took coffee, and the senator had water. They talked awhile and the senator asked each of them to tell him about their personal background. He began with the young lady and as she talked he appeared to be enthralled by her personal story. He relaxed and leaned his chair back and listened intently, occasionally asking a question. When she was concluding he asked about her matrimonial plans and she said that there was no man in her life except her father and that she intended to wait for just the right man. The senator smiled his approval and leaned back again. He was a handsome man in his fifties, rich, well bred, well groomed, well clothed, well connected, and head of one of the south's great law firms. At approximately forty-seven degrees into the lean the senator entered the zone. He instantly relinquished all concerns about his handsomeness, his wealth, his breeding, his grooming, his clothing, his connections, his national status, and even his incipient thoughts about the beautiful young lady seated across the table from him. He let out a loud grunting sound, not quite a yell, his chin jutted forward, his eyes bugged out, his mouth opened grotesquely; he first reached for non-existent handles in the air and then flailed about, moving both arms wildly in a circle, probably in an attempt to move his center of gravity forward during that terrible pause just past the forty-seven degree point and before his descent toward the floor accelerated. None of this worked. As he crashed to the floor his legs flew up and turned over the coffee table and spilled the beverages that were still on it including the pot of coffee and accompaniments, and he knocked over a floor lamp that he tried to grab on his way down. All this made a loud commotion that brought the senator's secretary and two or three others running in. The secretary helped the senator get up off the floor. He was breathing heavily, his hair was tussled, his suit was crumpled, and there was a gap where his two upper front teeth had been. He had somehow managed to spit out a partial plate and was now looking for it on the floor. Daddy and the young lady remained seated – what could they have done in a span of two to three seconds? They were both excruciatingly embarrassed for the senator and could only smile at him and his people. The senator never looked at them. The secretary glared at the two youngsters, as if they had caused this humiliating catastrophe, and walked the senator out of the room, telling him not to worry about his false teeth, that they would find them, and Daddy and the young lady got up and left. Daddy never got to complete his interview and neither of them got the job...

But back to the caboose.

The conductor yelled as the train came to a stop and all four men including the conductor climbed down out of the caboose to see what had happened. The engineer, a big, burly man, walked as fast as he could toward the rear of the train. He walked past the men and the caboose for another seventy-five yards or so and stepped down into the ditch by the tracks and bent down. He stood up and started walking back toward the men holding a huge mud turtle.

While the engineer was hustling back to where he had seen the mud turtle the conductor was grimacing and contorting from his rapidly augmenting pain, holding his groin and jumping like a young boy who had an uncontrollable need to pee. His entire front side had been scalded from his neck down, including his privates. As the engineer approached the men and the conductor saw the mud turtle and understood why the engineer had stopped the train, and precisely why he had suffered such an intensely painful scalding, which suffering was escalating moment by moment, Daddy said the conductor exclaimed to the engineer that he should never have stopped the train just to get a mud turtle, no matter how big he was. Daddy said the conductor expressed these sentiments to the engineer using a crescendoing stream of profanity and obscenities and other highly refined forms of invective. Daddy said the conductor even made references to the engineer's mother several times during his admonitions to the engineer, and even grouped the engineer and his family right in with several forms of livestock.

The other men were stunned; they had been working with the man for years and had always known him to be a rather religious man who regularly went to church no matter what town he was in. They had never heard him cuss, and they had never heard anybody take it to the level they were now experiencing even though they had both grown up on farms down in eastern North Carolina where profanity was just another dialect.

The engineer hardly seemed to hear the conductor as he walked past the men toward the front of the train with a big smile on his face, holding his turtle up for the men to see. Daddy said the conductor continued to yell at the engineer, but the engineer never turned around. He was so focused on his prize that he never realized what had happened to the conductor. When he got to his engine, he lifted the turtle up into the cab and laid it upside down on the floor and grabbed the handrail and pulled himself up into the cabin and closed the door.

Daddy said the conductor finally stopped yelling and cussing and started grimacing and contorting and moaning again, and finally just stood still, defeated. Daddy said he was almost catatonic by now and the men had to help him back into the caboose. The men could see that he was in extreme pain from the stiff wet overalls rubbing against his burns, so they helped him remove his overalls; they mopped up the coffee with one of the sheets from a bunk, and so that he would not be stark naked for the rest of the trip to Richmond they draped the other sheet from the bunk around his neck like a barber's cloth and then laid him on his back on the floor on the thin cotton mattress from the bunk; he didn't have the strength to climb into the elevated bunk, and he wouldn't let the men lift him up there.

The other men told Daddy to flag the engineer that all were aboard and the train could start moving again. Daddy looked around the caboose but he couldn't find the conductor's flag so he used the conductor's overalls, waving them up and down outside the caboose. The engineer apparently understood the signal because the train began to move forward. Daddy saw the conductor watching him use his overalls to signal the engineer. When their eyes met the conductor looked away in a daze.

A couple of hours later they pulled into Richmond. The conductor had moaned and groaned the whole way. When the train backed into its offloading spur and stopped, the men helped the conductor down out of the caboose and all three of them walked with him to the boarding house where they stayed when they were working the yards in Richmond, two blocks from the rail yard. Daddy said there were lots of people who were out and about, and they stared at the conductor as he slowly moved down the sidewalk with the bed sheet draped around him, which was highly unusual on a public sidewalk even down by the rail yard, but the conductor didn't seem to be aware of this because he was still in a daze, barely able to put one foot in front of the other. One of the men walked in step behind the conductor holding the sheet together so that the other people could not see the conductor's bare backside. Daddy was carrying his overalls and people also stared at the overalls and at Daddy. Daddy said it only later occurred to him that some of the people staring at the overalls surely must have been wondering if the conductor had experienced some sort of bowel accident, but nobody asked. They just stopped and stared; this was probably a first for all of these people.

The men eventually got the conductor up the front steps of the boarding house and to his room and into his bed. Every time he made the slightest move he moaned. The other men left and went out onto the front porch to sit and smoke while they waited for supper.

Daddy stayed in the room with the conductor and around dark, without thinking, Daddy asked him if he would like a cup of coffee. Daddy said the conductor gasped and started shaking and his eyes went wild for an instant and then he settled and stared straight ahead. Daddy said at that point he realized he probably shouldn't say anything about coffee for a while, at least not within hearing of the conductor.

The lady who ran the boarding house knocked on the door.

"It's me. Can I come in?

"Come on in."

She stepped in and stared at the conductor. He glanced at her and then looked away. He had been staying here in her boarding house for years. She had left middle Tennessee over twenty years before when she married a soldier boy from Richmond. He had got shot dead in a bar fight a few years back and she took the ten thousand dollars insurance proceeds and bought the boarding house.

"You'uns okay? I seen you'uns comin' up the steps an' him awearin' a bed sheet. Why wuz you wearing a bed sheet right out in broad daylight?"

Without waiting for an answer she looked at Daddy, "Why wuz you carrying his overalls? He ditn' soil hisself did he?"

"Ma'am?"

"Soil hisself – mess in his pants. He didn't mess in his pants did he?" She studied the conductor, looking him up and down. The conductor looked at her wild-eyed and quickly looked away, staring at the ceiling and breathing heavily.

"Yes ma'am, we're all okay except for him. Naw, I don't think he messed in his pants, but it's possible – I hadn't thought about that." Daddy glanced at the overalls and looked at his hands front and back, and then raised them to his nose. "He got burnt on the train comin' up here. He got scalded by a whole pot of live boilin' coffee. The whole pot poured right down the front of'im inside his overalls, and he didn't even have a shirt on or any undershorts."

The conductor glanced wildly at Daddy and breathed even more heavily.

"You shoulda seen it. It was horrible, him kickin' and screamin' and flailin' and slappin' around trying to beat the hot coffee off of'im."

Daddy looked at his hands again. "You know, come to think of it, he may have had an accident during all that jumping around and being scalded." Daddy didn't mention the turtle or the cussing.

The landlady stood with her mouth open staring at the conductor; she appeared to be trying to imagine the action in the caboose. The conductor glanced at Daddy again and then looked back at the ceiling, still breathing heavily.

"Well let me know if I can do anything for'im. You reckon he needs to go to the toilet?"

She studied him. He stared at the wall beyond the foot of his bed.

"Yon't me to bring you a chamber pot in here? You need to make water?" She spoke louder to him than she had been speaking to Daddy, perhaps thinking that the scalding had affected his hearing.

The conductor grimaced as he shifted slightly. He was still breathing heavily. "I don't believe I'd be able to make water right now even if I needed to," he gasped. "I don't know if I'll ever be able to make normal water again. I'd appreciate it if y'all would just leave me alone now and let me git some rest."

"You reckon we ought to call the doctor?"

"Naw, I ain't goin' to no doctor."

"Yon't me to git you one to come here?"

"I'm tellin ya, I just need to be left alone now so I can git some rest."

"You want your supper? Everbody else is already in there eatin'."

He didn't answer. He stared straight ahead.

"I'm comin'," Daddy said, "I'm hungry. That food smells good!"

Daddy started across the hall into the dining room, leaving the bedroom door open so he could hear the conductor call him if need be, and stopped in the middle of the hall. He looked down at his hands front and back and instead of going on into the dining room he turned and walked down the hall to the bathroom and gave his hands a thorough scrubbing with a chunk of lye soap. He then joined several other men at the dining room table, where there were bowls of fried chicken and vegetables of all sorts and hushpuppies and

biscuits and mashed potatoes and gravy, and although the
other two men had probably already briefly recounted the
events of that day, Daddy told these men a moment by moment account of what had happened, recounting in precise
detail the conductor's encounter with the boiling liquid and
his reaction to it as he was being scalded. The men began to
chuckle as they imagined that scene, but when Daddy got to
the part about the mud turtle and the cussing they started
howling, and when he finally described the scene of the conductor walking through town naked as a jay bird except for
the bed sheet wrapped around him, and the one man walking in step behind him holding the sheet closed, and the
crowds gathering and staring at him, they couldn't talk or eat
they were laughing so hard.

After a few minutes the landlady came to the dining
room door that was just across the hall from the conductor's
bedroom door, which was still open, and told the men to
calm down for a minute – she had some good news for them.
Being the southern boys that they were, the men settled
down and politely obeyed, turning their attention to her.

"Y'all's engineer just brought me a big mud turtle with
his head cut off and I'm gittin ready to dress it now and I'm
gonna cook y'all some turtle soup for tomorrow night!"

The men looked at each other and yelled their approval
– what hardworking southern man didn't love turtle soup?
And at that moment from the conductor's bedroom came a
loud sobbing wail and then the sound of something crashing
to the floor. The landlady hurried into his room and found
the conductor still in bed, still partially covered, panting and
sweating heavily. The lamp and his bedside table lay on the
floor.

"What's wrong?" She stared at his groin area, which was
still covered by the sheet. "You hurtin' from not being able
to pass water?"

"You gonna cook that turtle in the kitchen?"

"Where else would I cook a turtle?"

"I gotta get outta here before you start cooking that turtle!"

"What for? You cain't even move. You cain't make water and you cain't walk and no telling what else you cain't do! What you got against that turtle?"

"Please don't cook that turtle tomorrow. I just need a few days to get well."

"I cain't do that. That'd be a waste of a whole lot of good turtle meat that'd go bad – it won't keep in the ice box. What you got against turtle soup now? You've eat it before rightchere in this house and loved it."

"Would you throw it away for an extra month's rent? I just don't believe I can stand the smell of that turtle cooking in the morning."

"I cain't do that. It's not my turtle to throw away. It belongs to y'all's engineer and he wants me to cook it. Besides, I'll bring you a bowl of it in here and you can eat it rightchere in this room. You won't have to go in yonder to eat. It'll give you some strength and perk you right up and that's what you need. I'll take care of ya." She kept glancing at his groin area. The sheet covered him to a couple of inches below his belly button, and above that she could see red raw flesh with skin peeling away.

"What happened to this lamp and this bedside table?"

The conductor was panting more heavily now. He looked at her and then quickly back at the ceiling. He was almost breathless. She stooped and lifted the table and put the lamp back in place.

"I'm gonna bring you that chamber pot in here when I finish cleaning that turtle. You ain't fit to even walk down the hall to the toilet. Now you just settle down and rest. I'll bring you some of that turtle soup tomorrow evenin' and you'll be better before you know it! I bet you anything that just smellin' it cookin' all day'll make you feel better. I'm gonna soak the meat in salt water with a little vinegar in it all night to take the stink out of it 'fore I start cooking it."

He gagged.

"I promise I'll bring you the first bowl of it!"

He gasped and closed his eyes.

"Now I got to get out there and dress'im 'fore dark. You need anything else other'n the chamber pot? I've even got a little bed pot for passing water in bed that I'll bring ya. Yont it now?"

He opened his eyes and glanced at her and then turned away and stared at the wall. She left the room. He closed his eyes and tried to sleep.

In a few minutes he could hear the sound of the hatchet coming from the back yard as she split the turtle's shell, chop, chop, chop. The men had finished eating and were back on the front porch smoking. The whacking of the hatchet became louder. Off in the distance a rooster crowed. He opened his eyes and the room was spinning... He sensed it before it started... He tried to rise but his legs wouldn't move... He felt the trickle and then the flow began... He yelled for the bed pot.

---

This was usually the end of the story because Daddy would be laughing so hard that he couldn't talk any more. Such was the case this evening; the whole crowd was in stitches when Mama stuck her head in the door. "Y'all come on in – supper's ready."

We all got up and went to the supper table. And even though the preacher was there, and the older gentleman from our church, Daddy said the mealtime prayer, after which we all dug in and the talking resumed.

During the meal the conversation got around to sports and Daddy remarked to the preacher that he looked very athletic and fit.

"Thanks, Jon. Nellie and I get together about three times a week at the Community Center to exercise with some other couples from church."

"Well, whatever you're doing it sure seems to be working. You look great."

"We do calisthenics and some weight lifting. We work

out as a group so we can encourage each other and keep up the pace. I think that really helps us stay with it."

My brother J.C. piped up and said, "Mama and Daddy work out about three times a week right here at the house. I can hear'em doing calisthenics in their bedroom after Jackson and I go to bed. And Mama always encourages Daddy, too." The idiot had never used the word calisthenics in his life.

During those years Mama and Daddy slept upstairs at the end of the hall and my brother and I slept in a room next to theirs. Their bedroom door was always closed at night and of course we were not allowed to open it without their permission. There were clothes closets between the rooms but we could still hear them talking and snoring in their room. Both of them snored, and both denied it.

My brother was two years younger than me and during those years I was convinced that he was an idiot (today he's our governor). He was born Jonathan Charles Steadings, but we called him J.C. He was named after Daddy except they didn't have the same middle name. He didn't like to be called Charles and we couldn't call him Jon or Jonathan because it would get too confusing around the house, so we all settled on J.C. and that was fine by him.

"What do you mean I encourage Daddy?" Mama asked J.C. She looked puzzled.

"Because I can hear you telling Daddy, 'Don't stop, Don't stop,' and ya'll keep on doing calisthenics for awhile. I can hear ya." J.C. was beaming – obviously proud of Mama and Daddy, and of his new word.

After a few moments a rooster crowed way off in the distance, gently piercing the silence with his bedtime crowing.

The sound of the crickets outside became almost deafening...

A dog barked somewhere.

J.C. and I looked around at everybody. Nobody was looking at anybody. Nobody was saying anything.

Daddy looked intently at the bowl of mashed potatoes.

The preacher and his wife looked at their plates silently; she shot a quick glance at the radiators and he studied the chandelier for a moment.

The older couple looked through the window at the beautiful street lights outside that were illuminating our street and sidewalk.

Mama looked like she was taking the flu. I'd never seen it come on that fast.

I watched Daddy as he looked harder at the bowl of mashed potatoes and pursed his lips.

After two or three minutes of absolute silence, the older man spoke up and told J.C. how it was good for us to keep on exercising all our lives because that's what keeps us in good shape. That and eating good meals like this and spending time together and encouraging one another. He was an elder at our church and had baptized me in the creek the year before.

"I still love to exercise regularly, J.C., yessiree, I shore do. But I cain't do calisthenics quite as much as I used to. Back in my day I'd sometimes do calisthenics two or three times a day."

Mama made a high-pitched sound and jumped up and rushed into the kitchen.

J.C. was still beaming. It was rare that adults addressed him with this degree of approbation.

The old man's wife glared at him and made a snorting sound. "That's been awhile," she grunted, as she jumped up and followed Mama into the kitchen.

By now practically comatose, Daddy continued to study the mashed potatoes, and the preacher and his wife resumed feeding and reloading as needed to keep a supply on their plates.

"Jon, would you please pass the mashed potatoes?" the old man asked merrily.

Daddy reached for the bowl of mashed potatoes in slow motion and handed it to him without looking at him or at anybody else at the table and the old gentleman thereupon spooned himself a massive serving of them and dug in.

"Man these mashed potatoes are good! I flat out believe they're the best I've ever eat."

When Mama and the elder's wife returned to the table with dessert and coffee it looked like they were both taking the flu, what with their red eyes and general demeanor. Nobody except the old man ate much dessert, which was unusual in this house, and after a few minutes of nobody looking at each other while they slurped their coffee, the guests left. As they were leaving, the old man motioned for J.C. to come over and give him a hug, which left J.C. almost beside himself. I don't believe I have ever seen J.C. as happy as he was that night.

I watched the old man walk with his wife to their car, whistling all the way, and when they got to the car, he jumped in front of his wife and opened her door for her and bowed with a sweep of his arm, motioning for her to enter.

After everybody left, Mama and Daddy moved J.C. and me to the first floor bedroom next to Daddy's study at the other end of the house. They completely switched the contents of the two bedrooms that night. It took us until almost midnight. J.C. and I had never stayed up that late except when we went to see Daddy's lawyer friend in Chicago and when we went down to New Orleans on vacation where we usually stayed with another one of Daddy's law school friends who was a state senator. J.C. and I kept asking what the big hurry was, but they just kept moving. Afterwards, when J.C. and I were in bed in our new room, I heard Mama crying and laughing at the same time and making shrieking noises way up in her bedroom at the other end of the house before I fell asleep. I had never heard this combination before. I didn't hear Daddy at all.

# THE TOWN

Our place was like many others in town, except a little larger than most, although certainly not the largest. We had about three acres and we were seven blocks from the courthouse square. Some people at the edge of town had plots of fifteen or twenty acres. We had chickens and always three or four pigs, and every year Daddy bought a young steer and put it on our pasture which was a little over an acre. Like everybody in town that I ever saw, we had a garden that gave us all the vegetables that we could possibly eat throughout the year, and then some. We were constantly giving away vegetables to people who came by but I don't know what they did with them because I'm sure they had gardens too – everybody in town did. Maybe they fed them to their pigs. We certainly did. And we had a little corn field, about a half acre, which with garden scraps and kitchen slops, including our dishwater, fed our hogs right up to hog killing in November or December every year. Mama used lye soap for washing the dishes, and the hog swill that we made with it wormed the hogs. They loved it, and we had healthy hogs.

The old aristocratic houses were mostly within a block or two of the square and from there on out to the edge of town were generally smaller houses on progressively larger plots of land; occasionally some of the younger generation who had made or come into money would build a big house out toward the edge of town on a big piece of land and would run their various enterprises from there. Most had domestic servants who resided in small but comfortable houses on the estate.

On the other side of the square from the old money, down toward the railroad, lived most of the white people in our town. Just beyond the railroad was a narrow band of shacks occupied by the less fortunate whites among us, and just beyond them were situated the first small Negro holdings, the beginning of Free Town. A progression of affluence similar to the white side of town could be observed as one traveled away from the railroad tracks through Free Town toward its outer edge. But almost without exception all these holdings, large and small, had one thing in common: they all produced food. Every one of them had a garden beside the house or behind the house, or both; and most of them had some form of livestock, even if it was only a dozen or so hens, and maybe a milk goat or a hutch of rabbits. Two does and a buck could easily provide a family with three hundred pounds of rabbit meat a year.

Occasionally people would move to the mountain from up north, or from down south where they had moved to escape the cold weather and found it too hot down there. One evening a couple of these outsiders, a woman and her husband, came to one of our monthly city council meetings, which were always well attended by many of our townsmen, and during the public statements part of the meeting asked to be heard on a matter they said they were very concerned about. The lady read from a prepared statement that she had written out.

"Council Members, my husband and I want to bring something to your attention that has been troubling us since we moved to this town.

"We moved down here three years ago. In the town where we lived before moving here it was illegal to keep livestock on your property if it was inside the city limits. The health department had done some studies of the dangers of keeping livestock in populated areas, especially chickens and hogs.

"My husband and I believe the time has come for this town to pass an ordinance prohibiting the keeping of any kind of livestock within the city limits, for the same reasons that many cities have passed such ordinances, namely the public health. We also believe the town would smell a lot cleaner without livestock in everybody's back yard, and people wouldn't be bothered by the incessant crowing of roosters. They crow throughout the day and night here, and the whole town has a very unpleasant smell. Thank you."

The mayor thanked the lady and asked if there was any discussion from the council or if any of the council members had any questions. The council members sat there and looked at the lady. The mayor sat there and looked at the lady. The lady stood at the podium and looked at the council and the mayor. The mayor waited, still looking at the lady. For a full two minutes nobody said anything. Somebody coughed. The lady looked uncomfortable. Two minutes is a long, long time when everybody in the room is staring at you. Finally the mayor looked at the members to his right and his left and then he spoke.

"Ma'am, there's not a snowball's chance in hell that this council will ever pass such an ordinance. We've just come through what a lot of folks call the worst depression this country's ever seen, but nobody in this town or on this mountain starved. They didn't even get really hungry. There was very little money around, but our babies still got fat. In fact, every family in town had meat on the table when they wanted it. They had vegetables galore and those vegetables grew so plentifully because the folks here in town used their cow manure and their hog manure and their chicken and rabbit manure to fertilize their gardens. Our people had milk and clabber and cream and butter. They had fresh eggs every day of the year. Some people may think manure stinks, but here on the mountain we think it is one of the sweetest fragrances in the world. And I doubt that you could find a single person here in town that really hears the roosters crowing, much less being bothered by'em. In fact they'd probably miss the crowing if we didn't have'em.

"We're mighty proud to have ya'll as neighbors – we

always try to make outsiders feel welcome here – and we certainly don't expect you and your husband to bother with keeping any livestock in your backyard, but we won't be telling our people that they can't keep a cow and some pigs and some chickens on their little places here in town. And if you need any country cured ham or bacon or stuffed sausage or eggs, there's plenty of folks here in town that will be glad to sell you some. Just this morning my wife was talking about what in the world we're gonna do with all these extra eggs we've got. If you and your husband need some just drop by the house and she'll fix you right up.

"As always, Ma'am, you're welcome to write up a petition and have two hundred voters sign it to force us to vote on an ordinance, but I am pretty sure that none of these councilmen is gonna do it by bringing a motion before the council. And frankly I doubt that you could find ten people in this town that would sign a petition. Again we want to thank you Ma'am, for participating in our democratic process here on the mountain, and you come speak to us any time you take a notion to."

Again there was silence in the room. And then everybody in the audience started clapping. If the lady was uncomfortable during the silence that preceded this speech, she was now downright beaten. She and her husband walked out of the council room and to my knowledge never returned. A couple of years later they moved somewhere and nobody on the mountain ever heard from them or missed them. People in town still have their pigs and cows and chickens, and until he died Daddy fattened a steer every year on his little one acre pasture.

# BILLY MATSON

I met Billy Matson one summer afternoon when Mama sent me to the store for some corn meal. A light rain was falling as I rode my bicycle to the store. Billy was there and we said howdy and Mr. Burnham introduced me to him and Billy asked me if I wanted to see where he lived. I said yeah and we went outside to the side of the store, walked through the garden and stepped into a chicken house. Some people said Billy was homeless, but that was not true. Billy's home was the chicken house behind Burnham's store, which was right next to the sheriff's house. That is, it had been a chicken house in the past, but when Billy showed up at the store one day several months earlier asking if he could do any work around the store for some baloney and bread, Mr. Burnham engaged him in conversation and found out that he had just got into town and didn't have a place to stay. Mr. Burnam told him he could stay there in the chicken house, and he could help him around the store some if he wanted to. He could sweep the floor and do other odd jobs in the store, and he could help tend the garden that supplied some of the greens and other vegetables that Mr. Burnham sold in his store. What little family Billy had were miles away and years ago; he told Mr. Burnam that he would be happy to help around the store and have food to eat and a place to stay. Mr. Burnam also gave him a couple of dollars each week for spending money, which was quite generous at the time.

The door where the chickens used to enter was not more than three feet high. There was a human door at the other end of the house but Billy liked to use the chicken door sometimes, just for the novelty of it. The chicken entrance faced the sheriff's house next door. Mr. Burnham had removed the roosts and repaired the roof and once inside Billy had a shelter from the rain. The floor had been dirt, but Billy and Mr. Burnham had put in a wood floor. Billy had some quilts and blankets on an old mattress, and Burnam had built a wooden frame about a foot and a half off the floor for a bed. There was one chair, one small table, and no other furniture of any kind except for two wooden crates. The only way Billy could see outside was to look through the small glass window in the human door or stand and look through the air vents in the wall near the ceiling of the chicken house. There were two of these at the lower end of the ceiling and two at the higher end. Each vent was about two feet wide and three or four inches high. Each vent could be closed with a hinged board when the weather was cold outside. I stood on a crate and looked out through a vent. I couldn't see the front door of the store but I could see the garden and the gravel parking lot in front of the store. I could see the sheriff's back porch through the vent on the opposite side. All in all, I thought Billy had a pretty nice place to stay even if he didn't have any windows. Mr. Burnham had even put in a little wood heater and had run a stove pipe through the wall and up the outside wall to a height of about two feet above the top part of the roof.

When we got inside, we sat on the wooden crates and Billy pulled a package of wieners from a paper sack that he had brought with him. He opened the package and held it toward me.

"Yont a weenie?"

"Sure."

I watched him eat, and he looked like he enjoyed every bite. He held each wiener in front of his face and examined it closely before taking a bite. We ate three wieners apiece.

"You go to school?" I asked.

"Naw, it's been awhile."

"How old are you?"

"Sebnteen."

I saw a stack of newspapers on the floor. "You read them newspapers?"

"Yep, Mr. Burnham gives me one ever Wednesday and Sa'rday just before he closes. I read'em front to back the day atter I git'em. Don't hardly have enough light to read'em that same night." He had one small kerosene lamp which he hung from a hook in the ceiling.

"Does that wood heater keep you warm?" It was the tiniest heater I had ever seen.

"It'll run you outta here. Only thing is it don't burn all night. If I don't git up and feed it durin' the night I have to restart the far in the mornin'. I can even cook on it."

We talked for a few more minutes and then went outside through the human door. Billy walked around to the front of the store and went inside and I went home, thinking about the various forts that I had built in the woods and how Billy was actually living in his fort. That evening I asked Mama and Daddy if I could spend the night in the barn and they let me do it.

# THE ROSE AND THE RATTLER

One morning that summer when the dew was still on the roses, and the early morning sun made the dew droplets sparkle like tiny diamonds, Mama worked in her flower beds outside. She loved to see dew on the roses and to smell them at that time of day. She was putting down some mulch under a patch of roses that she had in the side yard. As she reached under a bush to push some mulch around to even it out, she heard what sounded like a cricket and felt a thump and a sharp sting on her forearm, about three or four inches below her elbow. Startled, she yelped and looked closely under the bush and saw a timber rattler ready to strike again. She jumped back and yelled for me and rushed toward the front porch. J.C. and I were playing on the other side of the house and I could tell something was wrong by the way Mama yelled for me.

She called again and I got to the front porch about the same time she did.

"I just got snake bit!" she yelled.

"Where?"

"Right here on my arm. Go call Daddy and tell'im to come get me, right now!"

I ran to the phone and called Daddy's office and told his secretary what had happened and hung up. I ran back to Mama and she was already tying a headscarf around her arm just below her elbow using her good arm and her teeth.

"Finish tying this knot here," she said, "and then stick these shears through it and start twisting. I'll tell you when to stop."

I tied the knot and started twisting.

She grimaced. "That's tight enough. Daddy ought to be here in a minute." She was breathing heavily.

A couple of minutes later Daddy sped into the driveway and jumped out of the car and reached out and took Mama's hand.

"That there's a real snake bite right there," he said excitedly. "Let's get you in the car right now!"

Daddy helped Mama get in the front and I jumped in the back seat and we headed for the hospital.

When we pulled up to the emergency entrance, Dr. Allison was the only doctor at the hospital and we could see him down the hall in the colored people's area.

"We don't have a doctor here, but I can get one here in about ten minutes," said the duty nurse.

"What do you think he is?" Daddy asked, pointing to Dr. Allison.

"But he's a Negro, Judge!"

Daddy just ignored her and took Mama by the arm and walked up to Dr. Allison and told him that Mama had just been bitten by a rattler. Dr. Allison helped Mama take a seat. He examined the wound and the tourniquet.

"We'll leave that tourniquet as it is for just a moment until I inject a serum to start counteracting the venom."

A nurse had already fetched the serum and a syringe and needle. Dr. Allison filled the syringe and gently administered the injection as Mama sat quietly and watched.

"You're going to be a sick lady for a couple of days and there'll be serious swelling and pain so I'd recommend that you stay here at least until tomorrow so we can keep you under constant observation and keep you as comfortable as possible."

He loosened the tourniquet and within a few minutes she said she was feeling nauseous.

"I'll go ahead and admit you and we'll get you a room over on the other side. Who's your doctor?"

Daddy looked at Mama and she nodded. "You are!"

snapped Daddy, "and Molly'll take a room over in this section since this is where you are." Dr. Allison looked thoughtfully at both of them.

"Are you sure about this? This will be a first, and you know there will be consequences."

Mama and Daddy looked at each other again.

"We're sure," said Daddy.

The doctor called a colored nurse who arrived with a wheelchair. "Let's just ease you right down in this chair and we'll get you right into a bed," she said. She smiled at Mama and placed her black hand on Mama's hand. "We're gonna take good care of you sweetheart."

Mama smiled back at her. "I know you will." And down the hall they went. Thus occurred what was probably one of the first instances of racial activism on the mountain. Because she was so sick Mama ended up spending three days there under Dr. Allison's care, and for weeks afterward the mountain was abuzz with talk about how the judge of all people had put his wife in the nigger section of the hospital and had used the nigger doctor to treat her. As far as I could tell, this never seemed to bother either Daddy or Mama. In fact, if anything, they seemed to enjoy it.

As for myself, I've often thought about the contrast between that beautiful rose and that deadly serpent beneath it, and how that timber rattler's bite that morning figured in a series of events that would eventually change the whole mountain.

# TAMMY ALLISON

Two weeks after Mama and Daddy moved J.C. and me to the downstairs bedroom, and while Mama was recuperating from her snakebite, we had the local finals of the state-wide music competition sponsored by our state arts council. Louise Fulton was in my class at school and she played piano. She had been playing ever since I met her back in first grade and by the time we were twelve, this summer, she played exceptionally well. We took it for granted that she would win the local competition and would represent our school in the Regionals. She had had lessons twice a week for all those years, and she practiced several hours every day. She had a very nice piano. Louise's daddy was a surgeon.

"I'm going to play Piano Sonata No. 14 in C-sharp minor, by Ludwig van Beethoven," she had told me one day about a month before the competition in late August. I could feel my face starting to flush, and my chest and my stomach began to ache. I had been in love with her much of the time since we were five. We were going on thirteen now.

"He called it *Quasi una fantasia*, but now we call it *Moonlight Sonata*."

I was having trouble breathing.

"And I'm going to get to play *my* piano at the competition next month because Daddy's lending the Arts Council my piano since they don't have a really good one. He's even paying to have it moved over there for the weekend of the competition. Isn't that nice?"

"That's very nice of your daddy."

Nobody in our school could even come close to playing as well as Louise, but word was starting to go around that there was a girl from the colored school that could give Louise some serious competition. Her name was Tammy Allison, and her daddy was a surgeon too, but he just operated on colored people unless there was a major emergency when the white surgeons were not available. Our hospital had a separate wing for colored people, and Tammy's daddy couldn't go into other parts of the hospital. Louise's daddy operated on white people and colored people and he had access to the entire hospital.

School started back the second Monday in September, and the competition was that weekend. On Friday night kids from within each school competed against each other, and on Saturday night the winner and runner up from the white school competed against the winner and the runner up from the colored school. As usual the colored people had to sit at the back of the auditorium each night.

Louise got on stage and played *Moonlight Sonata.* She was masterful and easily won in the white school competition.

Most of the white people stayed for the colored school competition out of curiosity. A couple of kids played their pieces and people were beginning to enjoy themselves.

A colored boy walked onto the stage and played and when he had finished everybody clapped politely. Even the white people seemed enthusiastic. The boy took his bows and walked back to his seat and then Tammy Allison walked up onto the stage and touched the piano. All of the contestants had practiced on it earlier in the day. She turned to the audience and curtsied and took her seat. There was a hush in the auditorium; everyone knew that this was the girl that everybody had been talking about.

Tammy Allison was five years old when she began piano lessons. Her parents were living in Boston where her father was in his last months of medical school. By the time they moved to the mountain after his internship and surgical residency, Tammy was playing four or five hours a day every day of the week. She got up early, often waking her parents with her music at five-thirty in the morning. She often played them to sleep in the evening. Tonight for the first time she would play to a primarily white audience. The competition master stood and announced that Tammy would be playing a piece that she had composed herself.

The audience was quiet. Tammy began playing and I'm here to say that stars fell on our mountain that night. For a moment we were stunned, and then we were all one, transported by her music, utterly amazed. She stopped and stood and curtsied, and there was no applause, nothing, just silence. Finally I heard someone behind me where the colored folk were sitting start to weep softly, and Tammy curtsied again. Then a white lady near the front stood and lifted up her hands for a moment like some people do in some of the churches and started clapping slowly, above her head, and others began to follow until everyone in the auditorium was standing and clapping and yelling, and Tammy curtsied a few more times and walked off the stage.

I had never seen a white person applaud a colored person for anything on this mountain. I had seen it in Chicago when we took a vacation up there to visit Daddy's law school buddy, Luigi, and in New Orleans when I went down there with Mama and Daddy, but not here. I don't think anybody had ever seen that happen here. It was clear who was going to be competing Saturday night.

The next evening the auditorium was packed. Louise played first and then Tammy played, the same piece she had played the night before, and there was just no question who had won. There was some commotion down where Louise's parents were sitting. Before Tammy even finished her curtsies to wild applause, some men were on the stage removing the piano. One of them told her to move over and bumped her with his arm. She looked startled. She curtsied once more and left the stage.

The competition master stepped up onto the stage and asked for the audience's attention.

"Ladies and gentlemen, you're the judges of the competition tonight. Please vote by applause when I call each musician's name."

They chose the winners among the younger musicians first, and finally the time came to decide who had won in the senior category. Louise Fulton and Tammy Allison were sitting on the front row. Tammy appeared nervous and anxious as she waited for the vote; Louise appeared smug and confident, smiling as she looked at the huge crowd of mostly white people behind her.

"Ladies and gentlemen, we'll now vote for the senior musicians. As you know that category has now been narrowed down to two finalists, Louise Fulton and Tammy Allison. As you have seen tonight, both of these young musicians are highly accomplished. The decision will be made by acclamation."

The master paused for a moment.

"Please vote by applause for Louise Fulton."

The people in the audience applauded vigorously and heartily for Louise Fulton.

"Please vote by applause for Tammy Allison."

If the applause for Louise was vigorous and loud, the applause for Tammy Allison was downright thunderous. Everybody in the audience except the Fulton family stood and applauded and shouted, and acclaimed their winner.

Before the applause had completely stopped the Fultons jumped up and left through a side door by the stage. With tears running down her cheeks Tammy stood and faced the audience and curtsied. The competition master stood by her facing the audience and declared her the winner, attempting to yell over the continuous applause by the crowd of mostly white people.

As we filed out I was angry at how the guy had bumped Tammy up there on the stage. But I had to move on. Our row was emptying and Mama and Daddy were herding me out.

When we left the building that night, we all knew that

Tammy would represent us in the Regionals and that Louise Fulton was a runner up for the first time in her life. This was new to us; Louise had always won every competition that she had ever entered. But now she had been eliminated. The only way she could represent us in the finals would be if something kept Tammy from competing.

# DR. ARNOLD FULTON III

The Fultons were back home and in shock. Arnold paced the house, talking to himself. He was the main surgeon among four on the mountain. How could these people do this to him and the daughter of their main surgeon? Fultons didn't lose piano competitions. They never had. Fultons didn't lose anything. This competition should have been judged by judges instead of by audience response. Half of them were just mountain rabble anyway. The audience acclamation was not a true measure of the performances. The best that could be said of it is that it just showed the public's infatuation with this new musician on the mountain. How dare they elevate a nigger girl above a Fulton?

He was born Arnold Fulton III, and like his father he was reared on this mountain. Like his father he had studied medicine and surgery in Richmond. After receiving his medical degree and doing a one-year internship in a Richmond hospital, Arnold moved to Mississippi to complete his surgical training. Five years later he returned to the mountain and started practicing with his father, who retired eight years later and dropped dead ten months after that, leaving Arnold, who was his only known issue, a huge bank account, an enviable portfolio of rock solid stocks and bonds, and several farms scattered around this mountain and adjacent ones.

Arnold's father had never bought a farm but had acquired them by foreclosing on deeds of trust given to him as collateral for notes signed by patients who didn't have the cash to pay for his surgical services. Some of these patients had died under the scalpel and some had died months later, and almost all had been the primary operators of the farms, and they had left family members who didn't know how to carry on and make the farms pay. Most of these patients were in a terminal condition before their surgery and were going to die soon anyway, whether they had surgery or not, but Arnold's father frequently encouraged these patients to give surgery a try. Most of them made it through surgery and died at their appointed time, but now instead of just dying at their appointed time a few months later, they had both kept their appointment with the hereafter *and* they had left the mountain owing Dr. Fulton Jr. a very sizable surgical bill in the form of a note that was collateralized by their farms, which note had been signed and properly authenticated before the surgery. Dr. Fulton was more than patient with the families, waiting until the notes became due to request any payment. Then, when these families defaulted on the notes, as they almost always did, Dr. Fulton promptly foreclosed. Folks said he had got himself twenty some farms by performing these last minute surgeries, but none of them from black folk or the Cherokee. These perspicacious folk invariably preferred to purchase their needed services for cash if they had it and elected to have the procedures performed, and in any event to leave whatever ground they owned to their issue rather than to the Fulton empire.

Once he acquired a farm, Arnold's father would then acquire himself a tenant for that farm, who in some cases might be one of the deceased's survivors who was somewhat familiar with the workings of the farm but didn't have the money to operate the farm without a backer. Arnold's father would advance the money for seed and fertilizer, and the tenant would do all the work, usually with the help of his family, and Dr. Fulton would split the proceeds of the farm's crop with his tenant when the crop came in.

This landlord-tenant method of farming was well settled in the law and it enabled the landowners to achieve some remarkable returns on their capital. By the time Arnold III took over the surgical practice, these tenants were almost slaves to him as they had been to his father because they could at least survive under their present condition as tenants but would starve if they left.

Arnold soon began to enjoy this sense of ownership of these tenant families. Of course they were not his slaves in the historical sense, but he had almost total control of their lives. In these times where could they go? They stayed just to be able to eat and have a place to live.

Arnold was good to them, as one might be good to his stable of horses that would be expected to augment his wealth. He managed his farms by driving around to each of them at least every two months, and having the tenants come into town to meet with him in a little office on his estate in alternate months. In this way he was able to keep aware of what he owned and what his tenants were doing. He kept detailed lists of the livestock on each farm and thus knew how many hogs and cows and horses and mules he owned in toto.

One interesting thing about Arnold was that he wouldn't participate in his own hog killings. In late fall, when the weather got cold and stayed cold, the yearly hog killing ritual began. All over the mountain the hogs that had spent spring, summer and early fall processing table scraps, and garden trimmings and surpluses, and corn, and whatever they rooted from the ground, now departed this world, and their carcasses were parsed into hams and shoulders and sausage and liver pudding and souse meat, a gelatinous terrine also known as hog's head cheese because it was made from the hog's ears and snout and the root of the tongue and the skin from the head.

As soon as they were shot and bled the farmers scalded the hogs; this caused the hairs to turn loose for a few moments during which time the farmers quickly scraped the hairs off the carcass; the farmers then hung the hogs upside down by their hamstrings and disemboweled them. Their guts became chitlins and sausage casings and dog food; a

portion of their livers were made into liver pudding that
same night, and their lungs were cut into small pieces and
cooled and salted and cooked into lights and mixed with
small cuts of liver to become liver and lights hash, which
when stewed with onions produced a remarkable study in
buccal textural contrasts: one bite would produce a firm
granular resistance before disintegrating; that bite was a
piece of cooked liver, and the next – a piece of light, or lung
– would produce the sensation of biting into a chunk of
sponge. In those days a liver and lights hash was the delight
of many a toothless citizen in our parts.

Hog killing was a merry time on the mountain. It was
always done after the onset of winter, when the days stayed
cold. It was a time of provisioning, of ensuring the availabil-
ity of meat for the year to come, and of lard for frying chickens and fish, and for shortening biscuit flour, and for making
ointments of various sorts to treat the dermatological ills and
cuts and bruises and burns that might visit one during the
struggles and vicissitudes of the year to come. It was a time
of community, of visiting and helping one another. A family
hog killing would be attended by neighboring families who
would spend the day assisting in the processing of the hogs.
There was always a wood fire burning, and there would be a
lard rendering pot suspended over the fire into which those
who were cutting the meat would toss fat trimmings, and
children would stir the pieces of fat with long wooden ladles
as the fat liquefied and slowly sizzled out of the chunks, and
the remainder in the bottom of the pot cooked down into
solids that the next day would be cracklins, which during the
weeks to come would find their way into cornbread and biscuits, and, sometimes, when no one was looking, directly
into one's mouth. There were few experiences on the mountain as sublime as eating a piece of perfectly rendered pig
cracklin with nothing else competing with it in the mouth.

But Arnold had his tenants do his hog killing for him
when they had their own hog killing, as had his father. One
cold day late in the fall, shortly after Arnold had returned to

the mountain to begin his surgical practice, some friends
persuaded him to participate in the hog killing on one of his
farms. He got through the shooting, bleeding, and scalding
without much problem, but when they hung the hog by the
hamstrings and with a sharp butcher knife made the disem-
boweling incision – first from outside in, just below the
crotch to create a hole big enough to get the hand and part
of the arm inside the abdominal cavity with the knife, then
the long incision from inside cutting outward and downward
so that no guts or organs were cut – and the guts and other
innards spilled down into the tub below, Arnold passed out.
His tenant revived him by wiping his face with cold wet tow-
els. As soon as he regained strength enough to drive, he left
the hog killing and never came near another one. When he
had gone, his tenant remarked that damned if he'd ever want
Arnold cuttin' on him or any of his; he believed he'd rather
have that nigger doctor cuttin' on him if any cuttin' had to be
done. How the hell could a man be a decent surgeon and not
be able to see guts moving around without faintin'?

———————

But the problem at the Fulton house tonight was not
about hog guts. It was about the roiling in Arnold's guts.

Blair Fulton had poured herself a tall glass of bourbon
and drank steadily, pursing her lips after every sip. She loved
bourbon. She sat in a stuffed leather chair in the parlor and
stared straight ahead while Arnold paced angrily throughout
the house.

Louise sat at the dining table, sobbing and pounding the
table. She could not believe that this had happened. Surely
this had to be a dream. It was not possible for her to lose a
piano competition. She had never lost one in all the seven
years that she had competed. And tonight it happened in
front of everybody on the mountain! She was immensely
embarrassed. How could she ever set foot out in public
again?

Their houseboy Jackson stood by the parlor door waiting for instructions. His sister cooked and kept house for the Fultons. She waited at the kitchen door. Normally at this time of night Jackson would be in his little house at the far end of the back yard, but because of the family crisis tonight he and his sister silently took their stations and waited. Even before the Fultons returned home word had reached Jackson and his sister that one of their own had defeated Louise in the competition, and they knew from years of serving this family that they would be expected to be in the house. They knew the Fultons would speak and act as if their servants were not present, as if they were not really members of the human race. But they also knew that if they were not present during this crisis, there would be trouble for both of them.

Blair despised Arnold. She had once loved him, but over the years she had come to hate the Fulton name – her own name now – and what it stood for, and she knew that she would never be intimate with him again. Those days were gone and they both knew it. But their relationship worked; it served each of them in the essentials and she found her love and satisfaction in the bourbon. Ah, the bourbon! How perfectly it mated with her Pall Mall cigarette. Surely nothing in this world could feel better than inhaling the smoke deeply into her lungs and chasing that with a fulsome swallow of this elixir of the mountain country and then inhaling deeply the alcoholic fumes that lingered in her mouth. She was gratified. She began to watch her husband pacing. She enjoyed this moment; what a pleasure to see Arnold suffering so. She didn't care that the nigger girl had won. She watched Louise, who was still sobbing. The nigger was better than her daughter. She was better than Louise by far. Everybody knew it. That's why she won. Blair was glad. This was God's doing. This family was evil. She inhaled and raised her head slightly to blow out the smoke, keeping her eyes on Louise. She enjoyed her daughter's distress. She smiled.

"Jackson, pour me some more bourbon."

"Yes Ma'am."

The big black man gently took her glass and her ashtray and returned after a moment with a fresh glass of whiskey and a clean ashtray. She had already lit another cigarette and was drawing deeply on it when he handed her the bourbon. Her fingers brushed his as she took the glass. She raised the glass to her lips and drank. She was satisfied. Life was good. The whiskey and the cigarette were all she needed. She knew in this moment that she didn't need Arnold as a man, and she didn't need Louise. She drew whiskey into her mouth and breathed deeply, inhaling the fumes of the alcohol before swallowing.

Jackson was again standing by the parlor door. Blair watched him watching the others. Arnold was still pacing, talking to himself, his hands by his side. They were a surgeon's hands, not much different from the hands of a piano player. She looked at Louise's hands, pounding on the table. Jackson watched Arnold. Blair drank again and studied Jackson. She had often looked at him. Now, finally, in the presence of her husband and her daughter and her nigger maid, in all this turmoil and despair, this angst, she felt free to draw him to her and to press him tightly against her. She inhaled deeply on her cigarette and drank deeply again. Arnold paced and Louise sobbed, and Blair drew Jackson toward her and pressed him even tighter. She began to feel the onset of release. She knew Arnold and she knew there was evil aborning in this house, but this was too good to let that bother her now. This was good. Nothing could possibly be better than this. She drank again deeply and relaxed, exhaling softly.

"Ma'am, would you like a glass of juice?"

"No thank you, Jackson. But I would like just a little more whiskey, about half a glass for now, and two or three cubes of ice."

"Yes Ma'am."

She shivered, and smiled.

Arnold glared at Blair. He despised her. Why was she not distressed like Louise and him? How the hell could she just sit there and watch Louise and him suffering like this? Her tolerance for alcohol was incredible. By now she had to be drunk but she didn't show it except her eyes looked a little bloodshot. She even smiled at him when he paced through the parlor. She was disgusting. The idea of intimacy with her repulsed him – he would find his satisfaction without her, as he had many times in the last few years, and he knew she knew it and didn't care.

But what mattered now was fixing this problem with Louise. He had nurtured her in her music since she began to take lessons and had bought her a piano that only the rich could buy. He had given her everything that she ever needed or wanted, and she was clearly the best piano player on the mountain. The audience had made a wrong decision tonight; there was no way that little nigger, or any nigger, could be better than his daughter. What was wrong with these people? They had no common sense – surely they knew that there was no way he could allow this. He could not allow a nigger to win against Louise.

He saw Dr. Allison just about every day at the hospital, and he had observed some of his surgeries. What he saw was an exceptionally skilled surgeon at work, a man who had been educated at Harvard. He could have easily stayed in the northeast and worked in a high-paying practice there. But he had said he wanted to come back to the south and make a difference. As a member of the credentials committee at the hospital Arnold had seen Dr. Allison's transcripts and references. These were impeccable, but that was not the point; he was still a nigger and niggers don't prevail over Fultons on this mountain.

He began to form his plan. He had to be careful. He couldn't make the arrangements by telephone. That would require going through the operator to make the long distance call over to Barlow County, and that would be too risky because she would have to log the call, and might even listen to it. Years earlier his father had introduced him to a fixer in Barlow County whose services they would use from time to time when they needed to deal with a recalcitrant tenant when the law did not provide a remedy that would meet their needs, or when they ran into trouble foreclosing on a farm because of some deficiency in the loan documents when they had drafted the documents themselves without the help of a lawyer.

He would drive over there tonight, now. This would be the best time to go. All the niggers and Indians would be celebrating and all the white people would be at home running their mouths about how a nigger girl had won the competition, how she had beat that Fulton girl. It was solid dark now, and nobody would pay any mind if they saw him driving toward the hospital. In fact, that's what he would do. He would drive toward the hospital first and then turn around and head back in the direction of Barlow County, which would take him back past his house. Anyone seeing him would assume that he was driving to the hospital or driving home from the hospital. He would drive right back by his house and go see the fixer tonight. This thing had to be made right. There was no way he could allow a nigger to outdo his daughter.

# THE FIX

The music Regionals were going to be held two weeks from the night that Tammy Allison outplayed Louise Fulton and won the competition. The Friday night after Tammy won, just before midnight, deputy sheriff Burt Reedus noticed two cars from Barlow County parked in front of Dr. Fulton's house. He could see a light on in the house. Deputies on street patrol routinely checked the residences of important people in town. The deputy made a note of the tag numbers and when he completed his patrol and returned to the office he mentioned the Barlow County cars in his shift report and included the tag numbers. It was not that unusual for cars to be parked curbside in this part of town, but it was a bit unusual for them to be there this time of night, and even more unusual for them to be from another county.

———◆———

That same night, about one hour later, the hospital called Dr. Allison and told him that they had just received a call from the Rescue Squad and asked him to come to the hospital immediately to examine someone who was scheduled to arrive by ambulance at the colored section of the emergency department with acute abdominal pain and nausea. He got out of bed and dressed and left for the hospital. Moments after he left, two cars pulled up in front of the Allison house with their lights off. Four men got out of the cars and crept in the shadows to the house. The front door was locked, but one of the men quickly and silently picked the lock, and the men slipped inside.

The first one inside moved silently down the hall and found Mrs. Allison's room. The bedroom door was open and in the moonlit room he could see she was in bed. He stepped quickly to the bed and pressed his hand against her mouth. She moaned and struggled but could only make a muffled sound and she was unable to move – the man had control of her. Another man bound and gagged her; one stayed and held her and the three other men left her to find Tammy.

Tammy was asleep in her room. One of the men went straight to her and put his hand over her mouth and covered it with duct tape. He then lay across her so that she couldn't move. It was easy; he was a big man and she was a twelve-year-old girl. One man waited at the door. The third man grabbed her right hand and pulled it over to her bedside table. Tammy struggled and tried to pull her hand away but she was no match against the man's strength. He held a long piece of rough cut two by four board in his other hand. He raised it high above his head and slammed it down on her hand. He raised it again and slammed it down again and the bones made a cracking sound. He did it again. Tammy screamed but it was no more than a groan through the tape over her mouth. He tossed the board on the bed and the four men hurried out of the house and got in their cars and sped away.

In a daze Tammy pulled the duct tape off with her left hand and yelled for her mother. Her right hand was burning and pounding and she couldn't move it. No one came to her room. She crawled out of bed and went to her mother's room and took the duct tape off her mother's mouth and fainted.

Mrs. Allison looked at Tammy's right hand and screamed. Her hands were still tied but she ran to the front door and screamed until the lights went on in the house next door, and within a minute or so her neighbor was on her front porch taking the tape off her wrists. Charlie Caswell came running up to the porch and helped remove the tape. He told the neighbor to call the law.

The neighbor yelled back to his wife to call the sheriff and to bring him his gun; moments later a deputy pulled up to the house.

———◆———

Charlie Caswell was a night wanderer. In summer and winter he took late night walks in the neighborhoods around his house. Everybody in town knew Charlie and no one was alarmed by his nocturnal strolls. Everybody knew that Charlie and the judge were friends and often spent hours together on the judge's porch. Everybody knew that Charlie had books – books of his own – and that he also regularly visited the modest town library for hours at a time. Some people even speculated that Charlie was perhaps a writer of some sort.

One of Charlie's nocturnal beats was the neighborhood where Dr. Allison lived. It was about ten minutes walking time from his shack. This was the neighborhood where the upper class of the Negro population lived, the teachers and the undertaker and the two black doctors and the preachers and the one black lawyer on the mountain and a handful of other upper class Negroes. It was here that Charlie walked tonight. He was out later than usual, but the weather was perfect and he couldn't yet bring himself to go inside for the night.

There were only two streetlights in this part of town, neither of which was close enough to where Charlie now walked to pollute the bright light of the September moon that drew him outside at this time of the night. As he reached a corner he looked down the street in the direction of Dr. Allison's house. He was surprised to see two cars parked on the street a few yards from him, right in front of the doctor's house. Curious, he turned and walked toward them. These streets were always empty this time of night. Everybody who had a car parked in his own driveway, not on the street. He was very familiar with Dr. Allison's house, and he had never seen cars parked in front of it at night.

When Charlie reached the cars, in the light of the September full moon he could easily read the numbers on the license plates and the word Barlow. He took a pad and pencil from his shirt pocket and wrote down the numbers. He put the pad back in his pocket and walked on down the street. Just as he reached the corner, he heard a commotion behind him. He turned. Four men ran from Dr. Allison's house to the two cars. Instinctively he stepped behind a tree and watched them get into the cars and speed toward him. He kept the tree between himself and them and watched as they sped past.

He waited until they were out of sight and then started cautiously back toward Dr. Allison's house. As he approached he saw Mrs. Allison step out onto her porch and scream.

"They've hurt my baby!"

Charlie ran toward her. She was sobbing. The lights came on in the house next door and the neighbor stepped out in his pajamas and ran over to Mrs. Allison. He and Charlie pulled the duct tape off her hands, which were bound together in front of her and bound to her body by several wraps of the tape around her body.

———————

Dr. Allison walked into the emergency room and the duty nurse told him that the ambulance was not there yet. He asked her if she knew who had made the call. She said she didn't recognize the voice, but the caller said he was with the rescue squad and that he was calling from a pay phone. He waited. He chatted with the emergency room doctor for about fifteen minutes. Then two sheriff's deputies drove up and walked into the waiting area and one of them asked to speak to Dr. Allison. The doctor heard him and stepped over to him.

"Dr. Allison, I'm sorry to have to tell you this but your daughter's been hurt. An ambulance is bringing her here right now."

"My daughter? What happened?"

"I don't know. She should be here in just a minute. The sheriff told me and my partner to come over here and stay with you. He didn't give us any details. He just told us to get over here."

He heard the siren and seconds later the ambulance pulled up to the emergency room door. He rushed out to the ambulance and walked beside the gurney as they wheeled Tammy into the hospital and down the hall into the Negro section of the emergency department. Her right hand was wrapped with a white surgical towel. Dr. Allison watched as the white emergency room doctor gently unwrapped his daughter's hand. The surgical towel was crimson from his baby's blood, and her hand barely resembled a human hand. Her fingers were crushed and misshapen, and the bones of her hand were broken and bent and stuck through her flesh.

His stomach knotted and his heart pounded in his ears and a scream started deep within him. For his baby's sake he held it in.

# CHARLIE CASWELL

Charlie Caswell was a friend of mine – had been since I was a toddler. I often stopped by his shack down by the tracks just to pass time. Charlie was in his late twenties and did odd jobs around town to earn what little money he needed. During those years what fascinated me so much about Charlie was the way he lived physically. His needs were minimal. He had a roof and a couple of rooms that kept him dry and a little wood stove kept him comfortable in the winter. His house consisted of a front room and a back room. Each room had three windows in it. There was the front door and the back door and an outhouse where Charlie took care of his business. His parents had left him the land – about two acres – and he had the usual backyard livestock that gave him eggs, sausage, ham, side meat, milk and cream and clabber and butter. He probably never bought a vegetable. In his garden he grew field peas and potatoes and collards and mustard greens and lima beans and butter beans and tomatoes. He grew cucumbers and made his own pickles. He grew corn for himself and for his livestock, canning for himself while it was in the tender stage enough to supply him until the tender stage next year, and leaving the rest on the stalk until it dried and could be ground into cornmeal for him and cracked into scratch grain for his chickens or fed to his hogs. His chickens kept him in eggs all year, and he dried what food needed to be dried for storage, and he canned or cured the rest. He set enough eggs to keep his flock large enough to put chicken on his table whenever he wanted it.

But the amazing thing about all this was that Charlie

spent very little time doing it. It just didn't require much time. Most of the time Charlie was doing odd jobs around town to earn what little money he needed for coffee and flour, or reading, or walking around town, or sitting on the porch with Daddy discussing philosophy and politics and history and whatever else delighted them. He came to our house regularly to help Mama and Daddy with odd jobs around the place, but he came just about as often just to be there.

Charlie was smart – he was a reader and he read across a broad range of subjects. Our town had a modest library, and Charlie spent many hours there each week. He also bought books when he took trips out of town, and from time to time he would lend one to Daddy and then they would sit on the porch and discuss what they had read. Over the years Charlie and Daddy had become friends. They would often sit on our back porch and talk for hours. Charlie didn't really see Daddy as a judge. Daddy was just someone who had become his friend. Most people called Daddy "Judge", but Charlie called him by his first name, Jon. I think that pleased Daddy. Very few people on the mountain did that.

I even called Daddy Judge until I graduated from law school. I guess because that's what I heard others call him. In fact I didn't start calling him Daddy until after I was admitted to the bar. I had to make a conscious effort to switch because I felt weird addressing a judge as Judge – I felt like I was calling the judge Daddy. It took me several years to make the switch, and I still often refer to Daddy as the judge.

This morning I got there before Charlie got out of bed. I knocked on the door.

"Come on in. I'll be out in a minute."

The front room was the kitchen and living area. Charlie had a little table with two chairs and a kerosene cook stove at one side of the room and at the other side of the room against the wall there was an old sofa. There was a bookcase next to the sofa, filled with books. Charlie had made another bookcase with cement blocks and boards, and that was almost full of books.

I sat down at the table. I could smell the sofa and the walls and the floor and whatever he had cooked last night. It didn't smell bad – it just smelled like a shack that somebody lived in.

After a couple of minutes Charlie came out of his back room and said howdy.

"You hungry?"

"Naw I ate before I came over here."

"You want some coffee?"

"I believe I will." Mama and Daddy had started me on coffee when I was about three or four, at least as far back as I could remember. To my knowledge everybody on the mountain drank coffee from the time they were big enough to walk. They even drank it in the heat of the summer. Most people on the mountain claimed that drinking hot coffee in the summer would cool you down.

Charlie went over to his stove and I stepped over there to watch him fix his breakfast and the coffee. He had left a cast iron frying pan on the stove from the previous night and there was solidified grease in the pan from whatever he had fried. There were little footprints right through the middle of the grease, and patches about the size of the pad of my little finger where the mouse had licked the grease. Charlie made sure there were no mouse droppings in the grease.

"You sure you don't want a couple of eggs and some fat-back?"

"Naw, I'm full. Mama cooked us up a big breakfast just awhile ago."

Charlie took a match from the match holder hanging on a nail in the wall and struck it against the frame of the stove and lit the burner under the frying pan. With the same match he lit another burner and put a pot on it to boil some water. In about a minute the grease in the frying pan liquefied and the mouse tracks disappeared.

Charlie sliced several pieces of fatback from a chunk of salt-cured meat and put them in the water. After they had boiled for two or three minutes, long enough to cook some of the salt out, he removed the slices from the water, shook them off and put them in the hot grease. The frying meat popped and sizzled and filled the room with the smell of country cured meat. He filled his coffee pot and started it to perking on the stove. He took two cups from a shelf on the wall and handed one to me and nodded toward the coffee pot. "It'll be ready directly."

"So what brings you here this early in the mornin'?"

"I was just wondering if you heard what happened to that colored girl last night."

"Yep. In fact I was there with the neighbor that called the sheriff. I even gave the sheriff some Barlow County license plate numbers that I saw on two cars parked in front of the girl's house just before her mama came out screaming."

"They say somebody broke into her house last night and crushed her hand real bad."

"Yep. I saw it before the ambulance got there. When I saw her hand it made me want to throw up. Have you heard anything this morning?"

"Yeah. Word's getting around there might be trouble on the mountain. I heard the judge talking to somebody on the phone a little while ago and he told'em to watch out for trouble. Then he called one of the preachers over in Free Town and I could hear him asking the preacher to try to keep things calmed down for awhile."

Most of the colored people on the mountain lived in a community called Free Town. It was really just part of our town, but none of the white people lived over there and none of the colored people lived in the white part of town. Funny thing was, on the rest of the mountain when you got out of town, white people and colored people were just scattered around living on their little farms or their little patches of land next to each other, but they didn't do that in town. Here and there you might see a grouping of black folks' houses outside of town, but generally they were just scattered around like the white folks.

Charlie turned his meat and checked the coffee which

was percolating briskly now but it was still a little light.

I never knew Charlie to be prejudiced in any major way, but his house was between the white part of town and the colored part of town. He'd be in the middle if things got ugly. And of course the hifalutin white folks were at the far end of the white part of town, far away from Charlie's shack. We were hifalutin white folks but Daddy had always liked to go all around town and talk to folks in different parts of town and he always told me that people are people no matter what color they are. I had heard him talking to Mama telling her he didn't care much for this sheriff because he favored white folks over colored folks and he treated them differently and he called them niggers instead of colored folks or Negroes. Daddy always called them colored folks or Negroes. The sheriff's general approach was to whip up on colored people when his staff arrested them, but his deputies didn't do that nearly as much with the lower class white people unless they talked back to them, and they never did it to the people up near the hifalutin end of town, and of course they almost never arrested any of those people. And since the Cherokee shootings they hadn't been whipping up on the people in Cherokee Town.

Charlie took a fork and removed his fried meat from the pan and checked the coffee pot. "All right. It looks like the coffee's about right. Go ahead and pour yourself a cup."

"Thanks."

The coffee was good. I sipped it and thought about Tammy Allison. Before I left the house to come see Charlie I heard Daddy say word had got around real fast and that by breakfast time there was a dark mood all over town. Daddy told Mama he was worried. He told her a couple of the preachers had called him and said they were worried, that there were some people out in the middle of the streets in Free Town yelling and raising a commotion, and this was not normal.

Before I left Charlie's place that morning he told me it would probably be better to go straight home rather than wandering around Free Town on my bicycle, as I often did. I asked him why and he said, "It's too quiet over there."

"But the judge said they were stirring around making a fuss over there."

From Charlie's place on a normal day we could easily hear the sounds of human activities in Free Town, the edge of which was right across the tracks just beyond a row of houses where a few poor white families lived. I listened. He was right. The only sounds I heard were animal sounds, an occasional rooster crowing, a dog barking, a cow mooing. But no human voices, no pickup trucks, no radios.

"They're mad," he said. "They've settled down and started thinking – they all know what happened and who's behind it."

"Who's behind it?" I asked.

"Dr. Fulton – everybody knows it. Who else would want her hand busted up like that?"

"Then why don't they just try him and send him to prison?"

"Be patient. We'll see what happens. I imagine the judge is gonna have to deal with some serious trouble these next few days. If I don't see him today tell him I've got some evidence they might be interested in when they start investigatin'. But for now don't tell anybody else."

# THE SHERIFF

Sheriff Sam Bartlett was born and reared on the mountain and he knew just about every soul there. He knew most of them by name, and he knew enough about most families on the mountain and elsewhere in the county to get elected every four years hands down, despite his meanness. He was quoted as saying that he "knew how to keep the niggers in their place" and in fact he was able to keep most of them from voting by preventing them from registering to vote, or by preventing them from going to the polls if they were already registered. He accomplished this by sending his deputies out to arrest a few Negroes who were going to the polls and roughing them up and pressing false charges against them, thus intimidating the rest of those who were registered, or by arranging for white rabble to assault Negroes who attempted to register to vote.

As for the Cherokee, the sheriff made a deal with them that established a peace that continued until the sheriff's demise. It happened thus: Shortly after the Cherokee shot the legs out from under a crowd of the klansmen on Cherokee Ridge, Johnny Wolf and some of the Cherokee elders drove into town and paid their respects to the sheriff in his office. They told him that all of the Cherokee who had reached voting age were going to register to vote if they hadn't already done so and then they were going to vote in the next election. They told the sheriff that as long as he and his deputies didn't attempt to prevent them from exercising their rights as American citizens some of them would probably vote for him – although they certainly couldn't guarantee that – and the elders would do all they could to keep the younger Cherokee men who had the fury of youth still in them from killing him or any of his deputies. The sheriff considered this proposal and immediately agreed to it. He told the delegation that if anybody needed transportation to the polls or any other help just to let him know. The Cherokee replied that they probably had more wheels than the sheriff's department and all of the sheriff's friends put together at that moment and that they felt sure that they would be able to take care of their own transportation needs.

That settled the matter. There were no handshakes, no puffing on peace pipes or any of that nonsense, and from that meeting forward the sheriff and the Cherokee got along reasonably well. When his deputies needed to deal with a drunk Cherokee, as often as not they would drive him home rather than arrest him for public drunkenness; if the situation was so bad that they had to arrest him, they did it respectfully and did not beat him.

The sheriff had no such understanding with the black folks on the mountain. He was incapable of viewing them as equal to white people. To be fair, it should be noted that he did not view the poorer uneducated whites as the civic equals of the higher class whites on the mountain either. The bottom line is that over the years Sheriff Sam Bartlett was consistent in his relations with his constituents. He always had enough votes to keep getting reelected so he treated everyone according to the way he categorized them as human beings, or less, and was never troubled by such civic and constitutional concepts as social equality and equal justice.

He was a tough little fellow, wiry, slim, and somewhat shorter than the average man on the mountain. He kept his hair slicked back with a scented oily hair lotion. Although he was a fairly small man he was strong and wiry and handled himself well in any scrap that came his way.

About mid-afternoon a couple of days following the assault on Tammy Allison, Sheriff Bartlett told one of the deputies that he was wrapping it up for the day and would be back in the morning at his usual time, which was six o'clock. He said he probably wouldn't make it back to the office later in the evening as was his practice. He got in his patrol car and headed out toward the Fulton place, a twenty acre estate right at the edge of town. He turned his car into Dr. Fulton's driveway, got out of his car and went up on the porch and knocked on the front door. Dr. Fulton himself came to the door.

"How're you doin' Doc?"

"I'm doing fine Sheriff. Come in and sit a spell."

"I believe I will Doc. I need to talk to you about something."

The sheriff followed Dr. Fulton into his reading room. Fulton gestured toward a chair and they sat down. It was not unusual for the sheriff to pay a visit to the doctor at home. He frequently needed to ask the doctor questions about various criminal incidents in the county in which the doctor had provided medical or surgical services.

"I need to talk to you about this little girl that got her hands crushed the other night, Doc."

"Yeah, that was terrible. I can't imagine somebody breaking into a home and hurting a little girl like that, even if she is a nigger."

"Yeah Doc, that's right. And that's what I want to talk to you about."

The sheriff reached inside his jacket and pulled out an envelope.

"You know that little farm you got from the Swensons a couple of years ago?"

Fulton looked at the sheriff for a moment, a puzzled look on his face.

"Yes, I gave them every opportunity to pay their note before I foreclosed on it. Have you found some kind of a problem with the foreclosure?"

"No, there's no problem at all with those foreclosure papers, Doc. I've gone through the file and as far as I can tell you've got full clear title to that little farm, all two hundred and thirty acres of it. House, barns, sheds, and all. You even own the equipment and the livestock."

"So what's the problem Sheriff?"

"Doc, I'll tell you, the problem is with some other paperwork that I come across at the office that really isn't related to the Swenson farm."

Arnold stared at him, still puzzled.

"I don't understand, Sheriff. You said a minute ago that you wanted to talk to me about the little girl who was injured, then you bring up the Swenson farm, and then you say there's some kind of problem with some paperwork that doesn't have anything to do with the Swenson farm! I don't seem to be able to follow you. It's been a long day. I think I'll have a drink. You off duty?"

"Yep. I've called it quits for the evening, unless somethin' comes up."

"Scotch, Bourbon, or Mountain Juice?"

"How old's that Mountain Juice?"

"I've got some that's ten years old. It rested in a charred oak barrel for eight years."

"You know Doc, I believe I'll have a little glass of that Mountain Juice."

Dr. Fulton left the room and returned shortly with two small glasses and a decanter almost full of a clear amber colored liquid. He filled both glasses with the Mountain Juice and handed one to Sheriff Bartlett and sat down.

The men sipped and looked into their glass. The sheriff felt the Mountain Juice warming his insides, and felt a pleasant sensation in his arms and back. He had never been very concerned about interfering with the bootleggers on his mountain. The only time he ever arrested anybody was when the Feds – the revenuers – would call and say they had some information about a still somewhere and they wanted the sheriff to help them find it. He would get enough information from them to figure out whom the still belonged to. He would then get in touch with the owner who would promptly remove all the current equipment and replace it with some old obsolete still parts that barely worked and fill it with a few gallons of mash. The revenuers and the sheriff's men would storm the site, break up the equipment, and pour out the liquor that had been planted in the old vat. Usually the owner saw to it that some poor soul was present when the law arrived, and he would be arrested and taken to jail from which he would emerge within an hour or so, as soon as the revenuers left town, not having been formally booked and thus having no record of the arrest. The arrestee would leave the jail ten dollars richer – this at a time when four dollars a day was a good day's wages – ostensibly bailed out on his own recognizance, although this was just smoke because he hadn't been booked in the first place, and the sheriff would leave his office that evening one hundred dollars richer, and of course with a quart jar or two of the owner's best mountain whiskey. Sheriff Bartlett had even learned to schedule these raids when he needed some extra money. This evening he drank some of the best Mountain Juice he had ever tasted.

"Well let me just show you the paperwork I'm having a problem with, Doc, and I think you'll understand." Bartlett handed the envelope to Dr. Fulton. There was nothing on the envelope.

Dr. Fulton removed two sheets of paper from the envelope and began reading. He read silently and then studied both pages. After two or three minutes he looked up at the sheriff.

"I believe I do understand the problem with the paperwork now Sam."

"Yes," said the sheriff.

"I take it this would be the carbon copy of the deputy's report countersigned by you when the deputy filed it, and of course you have the original in some secure place."

"That's right Arnold. I figure you should receive the original at the closing when you give me the deed. I signed the report the morning he filed it, but I didn't read it until later that morning when things got hot over in Nigger Town."

Burt came on early that afternoon after gettin' a little sleep, but I had already pulled the original and the copy."

The doctor looked down at the papers in his hand. The plate numbers of the two cars were clearly visible on the carbon copy of the report. The deputy had noted that they were Barlow County plates. Everybody on the mountain had already heard about the note that Charlie Caswell had reported to the sheriff.

"I take it that these are the same plate numbers as those that Charlie Caswell turned in?"

"The exact same numbers."

"When do you want to do it?"

"I figure first thing in the mornin' Arnold. We'll meet at Jack's for coffee and have the closing right there, just you and me."

"I'll need a couple of hours to get a lawyer from outside the county to draw up the deed, Sam."

"That's fine. You better have him draw up a note and a deed of trust for, say, twenty thousand, just so he'll think I'm buying it on time. That way word'll get around and people will think that I'm buying the place from you on credit and nobody will wonder where a low paid sheriff like me would get the money to buy one of the nicest farms on the mountain. But you'll need to go ahead and give me a signed release of the deed of trust and a second original of the note that you've already signed as paid in full."

"Of course. All right, I'll see you there in the morning."

"Good. You better let me have that copy back, Arnold. I may need it in case something goes wrong."

Dr. Fulton looked at the two sheets in his hand, hesitated, and then handed them to the sheriff, who put them back in the envelope and put it in his inside jacket pocket.

The following morning Sheriff Sam Bartlett and Dr. Arnold Fulton met at Jack's at ten o'clock and drank coffee together, which was nothing unusual, and exchanged their documents, also which was not unusual – patrons conducted a lot of business at Jack's practically every day. Arnold gave

the sheriff signed originals of everything the sheriff had re-
quested. Sam carefully reviewed all the papers. Everything
was in perfect order. Thus it was that Sam Bartlett acquired
the two hundred and thirty acre Swenson farm in fee simple,
with no real encumbrances, including all the farm equipment and livestock, and Arnold Fulton, III, as he saw it, acquired freedom from conviction, and prison, and the loss of
his medical license. Each man figured he had just conducted
some good business. Dr. Fulton drove from Jack's back to his
home and burned the original of Deputy Burt Reedus's two
page signed report in his fireplace. Sheriff Bartlett walked
over to the courthouse and registered his deed. The clerk
that handled the registration never gave it a second thought,
for the sheriff often came in and registered deeds that he had
acquired at a sheriff's sale because of a foreclosure or tax de-
linquency. And although the sheriff believed that he had
considered every possible thing that could go wrong, and
had provided for it, he was still uneasy because he was going
to have to deal with Burt Reedus because Burt knew without
any doubt whatsoever that he had put the shift report in the
sheriff's inbox the morning after the assault.

# DEPUTY BURT REEDUS

**B**urt Reedus's story was well known on the mountain. Before he became a deputy sheriff, Burt had got into some trouble and had appeared in Daddy's court. Burt had a nine-year-old daughter, and he was charged with felonious assault for beating his next door neighbor almost to death when he caught the man fondling his daughter's private parts. Burt beat the man senseless, breaking several of his ribs and some bones in his face. The man was in the hospital for several days and almost died. The man never even went back to his own house after he got out of the hospital.

The prosecutor wouldn't drop the case against Burt, claiming that Burt had gone way too far with the beating, and he wouldn't prosecute the neighbor because the man denied fondling Burt's daughter and the girl just wouldn't talk to the prosecutor's people about what happened. It didn't matter to the prosecutor that Burt swore under oath that he caught the son-of-a-bitch (he put that in his affidavit) with his hand in his daughter's pants. So instead of demanding a trial Burt pled guilty, which astonished the prosecutor, and when the time came for his sentencing the judge asked him if he wanted to say anything before he sentenced him.

Burt was irritated, and snapped at the judge. "I did it. I pled guilty. And I'd do exactly the same thing again if I had to. I don't have the slightest regret for what I did. Just go ahead and give me whatever you're gonna give me. Nobody's ever given me a break before and I'm not gonna ask you for one now. Sometimes the law just don't take care of the situation – a man has to take care of it himself."

The bailiffs glanced quickly at the judge. They had seen him get mad from time to time over the years. The judge stared at Burt, and the bailiffs looked at the floor and out the window. Burt looked straight back at the judge.

For a few moments the courtroom was quiet. People fanned themselves with the cardboard fans provided by the local funeral homes and the ceiling fans ticked.

The judge flipped through Burt's file and looked back up at him. A full minute passed, and Burt stood there looking at the judge.

Then the judge spoke. "Young man, you say nobody's ever given you a break. Well I'll tell you what. I've decided I'm going to give you a break."

"Sir?"

"I'm going to give you a break."

"I don't understand."

"Do you remember when you came in here and pled guilty I told you I would reserve acceptance of your guilty plea until the day of sentencing?"

"Yes Sir."

"Well, I've decided I am not going to accept your guilty plea today. I'm going to reset your sentencing hearing for one year from today."

"Sir?"

"You abide by the law and stay out of trouble, take care of your family, and stay at your job for a year and then come back in here. If you've done what you're supposed to do and stayed out of trouble, I'll dismiss this case and you won't have a criminal record. If you mess up I'm going to accept your plea and send you to prison. Do you understand?"

"Yes Sir."

"Do you have any questions?"

"No Sir. Thank you, Judge."

The judge nodded, stood, and turned to leave.

"All rise," said the bailiff.

Burt stayed out of trouble and took care of his family and worked hard, as he always had, and a year later he came back into court and the judge dismissed the case against him.

About two weeks after his case was dismissed Burt went to the sheriff's office and applied for a job as a deputy sheriff, and the sheriff hired him on the spot. Word got out that the sheriff had remarked to several people that anyone who could swing a fist like that he'd be proud to have on his team. Besides, everybody on the mountain except the prosecutor said they would have done the same thing that Burt did except that they would probably have gone ahead and killed the man, and the sheriff, knowing these people as he did, believed that with the mountain holding Burt in such high esteem, hiring him would shore up some votes in the next election, and it probably did.

# THE SPECIAL PROSECUTOR

Trouble continued to brew on the mountain following the assault on Tammy Allison. For five or six weeks the sheriff essentially ignored the assault, but the people did not. Louise Fulton had gone to the state finals and lost. Most of the people on the mountain were convinced that Arnold Fulton had arranged the assault on the little Negro girl. Even the white folk generally believed this and began to complain that the sheriff ought to be doing something about it. The sheriff hoped that the matter would just die down now that the Fulton girl had lost the final competition, but that did not happen.

Two days after the men crushed Tammy's hand Dr. Allison and his wife took her to Boston to a specialist who he hoped would be able to repair the broken bones so that she would be able someday to play the piano again. He hoped, but he knew there was little reason to hope. And the surgeons in Boston confirmed this as soon as they had examined their patient. He asked them to do all that they could and they said they would do their utmost, and he knew that that would probably not be enough. The men that had done this to Tammy had taken her life, not in the sense of extinguishing her existence but by preventing her from growing and becoming what she was destined to do and to be. The perpetrators had extinguished a light – they had stolen an essence, and by this the mountain had suffered an enormous loss. And when Dr. Allison and his family returned from Boston two weeks later and word got around that Tammy's gift had probably been taken from her forever, the people got madder.

And the people felt hopeless. The people in Free Town, and all the other black folk on the mountain, began to grumble about how the law was just for white folks and that there was no justice for them and never had been. Sure, justice would see that they got charged, convicted, and jailed or worse if it was brought to bear against them as wrongdoers, but justice was not available to them when they were the victims. It had always been that way. So now the elders of the black community felt that they were on the verge of losing control of the young black men – and even some of the young black women. These began to grumble that they were fed up with the way their folk were being treated – had always been treated – and with the fact that the law only helped the white people, and that the time had come to do something about it even if it meant spilling some blood. And these angry young black men and women reminded their elders that they had the guns and the ammunition to do it now, and if the elders didn't make something happen, then the angry young men and women would make something happen, and it wouldn't be pretty. The youth abandoned the deference that they normally accorded their elders, and the elders saw it and felt it, and they were alarmed and scared.

The black preachers had always been highly attuned to the sentiments of their people, and they now saw the crisis approaching. Their young men were gathering in groups around fires in back yards and vacant lots, and they were spending a lot more time there than was usual and there was more shouting coming from the groups than usual, and there was no laughter. There was no laughter in the homes of the black folk at breakfast or at supper when the families were gathered round the table. In the church meetings the preachers preached about the virtues of patience and said that the law would take its course, and their listeners looked at them and listened and did not respond. The elders didn't respond and the youth didn't respond. And then the preachers would leap and bounce and dance and yell and reach out for responsive participation from their people, seeking that rhythm that characterized the services of the black church, but there was no rhythm and the audience did not respond. The preachers augmented the effort and worked themselves into a sweat but they did not hear "Amen," "That's right," Preach on brother!" "Praise the Lord!"

The preachers met on Monday and agreed that they should seek a meeting with the judge as soon as possible. Things were getting out of control. One of them went to the judge's secretary, explained the purpose of his visit, and asked if the judge could meet with them. She stepped into the judge's office and came back a moment later.

"He can meet with you tomorrow morning at seven if that will work for you."

The next morning the preachers and the judge gathered in his office. They told the judge that there was trouble brewing in the black community and that they were losing control.

"We cain't get the spirit goin' in church Judge," said one of them. "You know how our folks get a lot more involved in our preaching than you white folks do in church. Well our colored folks are what you might say disengaged Judge. We start the rhythm and they don't finish it. We preach and they don't talk back – they don't respond. That means somethin's bad wrong. We been tellin'em to let the law take its course with this trouble with Miss Allison, but they just sit there and listen. They're listenin' Judge, but they ain't agreein'. And there ain't no singing to speak of. It's awful."

The judge listened carefully, studying the men seated with him. He had arranged several chairs around a coffee table in his office and he had taken one of them, choosing not to sit behind his desk. From time to time he attended services at the various colored churches, and he knew precisely what these men were talking about. He knew about the rhythm and the audience response and the give and take even in the singing.

Another of the men spoke up. "Somethin's gettin' ready to blow, Judge."

The judge had long appreciated the value of intuition. These men were leaders in a culture of their own, and they knew their constituents. He listened.

"Somebody's got to do something about this thing with Tammy Allison. If the sheriff would get an investigation goin' we think it would take some of the steam out of the problem for awhile. But nothin's happening as far as we can tell. If we could just get somethin' goin' we could probably get things calmed down some. But right now a lot of our people are talking trouble."

"I'll talk to the sheriff and the district attorney today or tomorrow. Let's meet again early Friday morning and I'll let you know where we are on this."

———◆———

Sam Bartlett and Tracy Walton, the District Attorney, sat at the judge's desk across from him. The judge believed the DA to be an honorable man, a view he did not hold with regard to the sheriff.

"Where are we on the Allison investigation? The attack happened a good five weeks ago, and the colored folks are getting pretty worked up because they don't see anything happening. I met with their preachers this morning and the situation doesn't look good."

The sheriff spoke. "There is no investigation Judge. We've got a case file open, but there's nothing to follow up on. Burt Reedus says he saw some cars from Barlow County parked in front of Arnold Fulton's house the night of the attack. He even says he wrote down their license plate numbers and put that in his shift report, but there ain't no shift report for that night. Now I'm not saying I don't believe Burt, but the bottom line is that the shift report is not there. And there's nothing else to go on, absolutely nothing."

"Have you talked to Dr. Fulton? Everybody on the mountain thinks he did it. Nobody else had a motive."

"Yes I have talked to Dr. Fulton, and he says he doesn't

know a thing about it. He even sympathizes with the little nigger girl – he said he thinks it's just awful what happened to her."

"What about the information that Charlie Caswell provided about what he saw that night? I personally handed you the paper that he sent over to my house that morning." The judge was disgusted.

"We've got what he gave us Judge, but when we called Barlow County about the plate numbers, they came back as stolen that same night. Both cars belonged to upstanding citizens of Barlow County. So there's nothing to go on there. You don't need to worry about that piece of paper judge. I've got it locked in my office safe. I even took a picture of it."

"How about you, Tracy?"

The District Attorney thought for a moment before he spoke. "Judge, I've thought about this long and hard. I've decided I can't prosecute this case. I feel like there's too much of a conflict there. Before I became DA Arnold had me do quite a bit of legal work for him. I just don't believe it would be right for me to turn on him now. Or at the very least I don't think the public would have faith in the prosecution since everybody knows I represented him in numerous matters, and still do occasionally."

"Well we can't just keep this thing at a standstill. The colored preachers are telling me that if we don't get something started soon there's going to be major trouble, and they feel like they've lost control. Y'all know as well as I do that if the preachers lose control, we're in trouble."

The DA thought for a moment. "Well, I guess the only appropriate way to proceed is for me to write you a letter recusing myself, and asking you to assign a special prosecutor to the case."

The judge looked at the sheriff for his input, but the sheriff shook his head and said nothing.

"All right. That's what I'm going to do. Date your letter today and make sure I have it by tomorrow. I'll call the DA over in Jefferson County this afternoon and see who he's got that could handle this prosecution. Sheriff, I think you need to turn your office upside down and find that shift report."

"Yes Sir, I'll do that Judge. We've already done that twice, but we'll do it again."

"Don't forget Sheriff, the colored folks have about as many guns over in Free Town now as we have on this side, thanks to our Cherokee brethren. We need to keep this investigation going and we need to make sure the public knows about it. We don't want a war here on the mountain and it looks like one is getting ready to happen. Whether you like it or not, we need some good public relations right now."

The sheriff left the meeting and went straight to his home. He removed the copy of the shift report from a drawer in his desk and put it in a plain envelope and wrote Burt Reedus's name on the outside. He went to his closet and put the envelope in the inside breast pocket of one of his coats and left it in the closet. It should be as safe there as any place he could think of. This carbon copy might come in handy again down the road if he ever needed a little extra money.

The sheriff then drove to his office and told his secretary and the two deputies there to tear the office apart if they had to, but find that shift report. After fiddling at his desk for a few minutes he went to Jack's Cafe for some lunch.

———•———

The sheriff's staff did not find the shift report. By Thursday the judge had appointed a special prosecutor from the neighboring judicial district and had met with him. Also on Thursday, after reflecting on the judge's reminder that Nigger Town was now very heavily armed, and further reflecting on the fact that if anything broke out the Cherokee would side with the niggers, the sheriff visited the newspaper office and the radio station and told a reporter at each place that there was an active ongoing investigation in the Tammy Allison case. He then told his secretary that he was going to go to Dr. Fulton's house to question him in the matter.

At two o'clock the sheriff drove to the Fulton house, parked his car in the driveway, and went up to the front door and knocked. Arnold led him into his reading room, and the two men sat.

"Arnold, I'd say you're probably gonna get indicted."

Arnold was startled – this had come out of nowhere. "What the hell are you talking about? I thought we had this covered!"

"It is covered. There's a big difference between an indictment and a conviction. Even with Burt's testimony, and he will testify, all they've got is the slimmest suggestion that you might have had the same two cars parked at your house as the ones that were identified at the Allison house. But it's only a suggestion because they can't match up the plate numbers. In all my years in this business, that would be the slimmest evidence that I've ever seen in an indicted case. But the bottom line is that I've got to do an investigation and I've got to make it look like I'm asking you some questions about what happened."

Arnold stared at Sam. He had to process this. "You want some whiskey?"

"I believe I would. It's been a rough day."

Arnold stepped out of the room and returned with a decanter and two glasses. He filled the glasses and handed one to the sheriff. They both drank deeply.

"So how's this gonna roll out Sam?" Arnold studied him. Sam appeared to be nervous, troubled, and this was completely out of the ordinary for him. Arnold watched him take another drink.

"Well, the judge has just appointed a special prosecutor from the next district over and he's gonna interview Burt this week. Burt's gonna tell him what he saw, but he's also gonna tell him that he can't remember the plate numbers. Then the prosecutor's gonna look at Charlie Caswell's piece of paper and he'll interview Charlie. Then he'll dig around and see if

he can find anything else – which he won't." Sam took another long drink and continued. "He'll know he doesn't have
much evidence to go on at all, not even good circumstantial
evidence, but he'll figure he's got a shot at an indictment,
and I figure that since the grand jury is gonna be made up
from folks here on the mountain, and since they all think you
did it, and they're all mad as hell at you, they'll probably in-
dict you even though the evidence isn't there. I think that's
what we're looking at." He took another deep drink and
emptied his glass. Arnold refilled it.

"So what'll happen then?"

"Well, I'd say now's about when you ought to be hirin'
you a lawyer. Once they've indicted you – which I would
think would be in three or four months – the case'll be set
for trial. I'd say they'd try it in the next term after the indictment. It's already November now so I'd say you're looking at a trial in August or September." Sam took two swal-
lows, almost as if he were drinking water, and stared at his
glass. He was beginning to feel the burden of his circumstances, and the whiskey knocked down the jagged edges.

Arnold studied the liquid in his glass. "Sam, you know
we're in this together don't you? If I go down you go down."

The sheriff drank again, emptying the second glass.
"You ain't goin' down Arnold. The only reason they're doing
this is to keep war from breakin' out. In the end it won't
amount to nothin'."

The men sat quietly for a few minutes. Sam's breathing
gradually became labored.

Arnold smiled. He was going to punish Sam. He poured
him another glass full of whiskey. The men sat in silence for
a few minutes.

"How's the farm goin' Sam?"

Arnold could tell the liquor was hitting hard. "Sgoin'
purdy good Doc. I believe we'll get in a good crop nex' year."
He emptied his glass again and rose unsteadily. "I better be
goin'. I'm gonna need a good night's sleep." He stumbled
out of the room and aimed at the front door. Twice he

braced himself against the wall as he moved toward the door. Arnold watched him and smiled. Sam pointed his hand at the door handle and missed. He tried again and grabbed it, using it to brace himself once again to keep from falling.

"Sam?" The sheriff turned and looked at Arnold, his eyes glazed and his mouth hanging open. He clung to the door handle, and swayed. He had drunk three full glasses of whiskey in less than twenty minutes. And these were not shot glasses. They were the glasses that Jackson's sister used to serve juice at breakfast every morning.

"Sam, remember – if I go down you go down."

Still swaying, Sam leaned his torso forward, pressing downward on the door handle. He turned his head sideways to look at Arnold. The door opened and Sam fell outward and down onto the porch. He clung to the handle and slowly pulled himself up.

"Ain't gonna nothin' come a this Doc. She wont nothin' but a little nigger girl then, and she ain't nothin' but a little nigger girl now. You ain't got nothin' to worry about. I'll take care of everything for ya."

Sam turned toward his car and saw two of them. He went down the steps sideways, holding the rail. At the bottom he sank to his knees and began to crawl to the car. The car began to move and the ground rose and lurched.

Arnold closed the door and smiled. Two hours later he called an ambulance and told them that the sheriff had passed out in his yard and that he had a hunch the sheriff might have low blood sugar.

Burt Reedus was just coming on duty when he heard the radio dispatcher talking to the ambulance driver. He and another deputy arrived at Arnold's house just as the ambulance was pulling into the driveway. The sheriff lay on the ground twenty or so feet from his car stretched out flat on his stomach with his head toward the car. He was snoring heavily and his cheek lay in a glob of vomit.

Arnold told the medics that he assumed the sheriff had intended to meet with him about something, but he didn't know what, and that the sheriff may have been there for some time before he noticed him lying in the yard. He said he had called for an ambulance the moment he discovered him lying there.

Burt watched the medics examine the sheriff and slide him onto the gurney and load him into the ambulance. He noticed another small patch of vomit between the sheriff and the house. He concluded that the sheriff was going toward his car, not away from it, when he passed out. He reeked of whiskey.

The two medics and the deputy who arrived with Burt took Sam straight to the emergency room and one of the medics, looking directly at the floor, told the attending physician that Dr. Fulton had suggested a diagnosis of low blood sugar. The other medic and the deputy studied the equipment in the room. The emergency room doctor examined the sheriff, who was still passed out and snoring, and concluded that he was drunk as a skunk. He wrote in the patient chart that the sheriff appeared to be hypoglycemic and that he had experienced a seizure and lost consciousness due to a low blood glucose level. He did not write anything about the vomit that the nurse had cleaned off the sheriff's face, nor about the intense smell of mountain whiskey that permeated the examining room.

The next edition of the newspaper came out two days later and reported that the sheriff had gone out to Dr. Fulton's house to question him about the Tammy Allison case, and had had a seizure due to low blood sugar and passed out as soon as he got out of his patrol car. The story reported that the sheriff would resume his questioning as soon as he had rested a few days and recovered his strength.

Burt wondered why the sheriff had gone to Dr. Fulton's house and had got drunk. He thought about his shift report. The disappearance was truly odd. He had never failed to submit a shift report in the six years that he had been a deputy, and he could go to the files and pull every one that he had ever filed during those six years, except this one. He went to the office and read the reports from the previous shifts that day before commencing his nightly patrol.

———— ◆ ————

Over the next two weeks, the prosecutor from Jefferson County spent six days in town with his investigator. They interviewed Charlie Caswell and got the sheriff to give them Charlie's note, which they reviewed and photographed. They interviewed Burt Reedus and questioned him in detail about the shift report and how he had written it and filed it. Burt told them that it was not his practice to file the reports in the sense of putting it into a file, but that he always put it in the sheriff's in-box on his desk. He assured them that he had not the slightest doubt about what he did with the report. He remembered the details of the report, but he could not remember the plate numbers. They assured him that they understood.

They interviewed the Allisons and several of their neighbors. The only remotely useful fruit of those interviews was that a couple of neighbors down the street were awakened by the sound of the speeding cars and could provide corroborating testimony about that part of the evidence; but they got nothing that would help them identify an assailant or link any individual to the crime, including Dr. Fulton. They interviewed Arnold's neighbors and got nothing.

They interviewed the house servants of the Fulton family, Jackson and his sister. Neither one of them was helpful other than saying that the Fulton family was very upset the night Louise lost the competition to Tammy Allison, but this was not the kind of evidence that would normally get somebody indicted. Arnold had been smart enough not to reveal his plans to anyone in his household, not even Blair.

They attempted to interview Arnold, but he had taken the sheriff's counsel and had hired Jeremy Brooks to represent him. Jeremy had told him not to talk to anyone about the case and not to answer any questions whatsoever.

The special prosecutor asked the court to convene the grand jury. He issued the required summons. Eighteen men from the county met in the courthouse and listened to the prosecutor's presentation. Charlie Caswell testified. He identified the note that he had written and told the grand jury about the two Barlow County cars and the four men, about how bright the moon was that night, and about hiding behind the tree and then hearing the scream and running up to the Allison house. Burt testified about the two Barlow County cars in front of the Fulton house and about the shift report and his inability to remember the license plate numbers. Jackson and his sister testified. They told the jurors that Arnold Fulton was very upset the night his daughter lost the competition, but that he never said anything about hurting anyone. The Allisons testified, their neighbors testified; the prosecutor called the ambulance driver and medics who had brought Tammy to the hospital; he called the switchboard operator who had connected Dr. Allison when he was called in for the abdominal emergency. She testified that the call had come from the hospital. She also testified that just minutes before she had connected the hospital to a call from a pay phone near the rescue squad's building. She assumed it was from the rescue squad.

The sheriff testified. He said he had complete trust in Burt Reedus, but that no matter what Burt said there was no shift report from him on his desk the morning after the attack. He said he didn't doubt Burt's testimony, but if Burt put it in his in-box, somebody took it out before he got to work that morning.

They subpoenaed Dr. Fulton, but he brought Jeremy with him, and although Jeremy could not go into the grand jury room, he told the prosecutor that his client was not going to testify based upon his rights under the Fifth Amendment to the United States Constitution. They called Arnold in anyway and he respectfully declined to answer any of the questions other than to identify himself. He appeared smug, and kept his cool. After several questions the prosecutor excused Arnold.

When he had presented all his witnesses the prosecutor presented his argument. He began with his strong points. He argued that nobody on the mountain had a motive to hurt Tammy Allison but Arnold Fulton. He reminded the jurors that Louise Fulton was the runner-up in the competition and that the only way she could go to the finals was if Tammy Allison, the winner, could not go. If Dr. Fulton could prevent Tammy from going to the competition, then his daughter would automatically be in the finals. But for that to happen he had to do something to keep Tammy from going. And that something was to incapacitate her.

He argued that it didn't matter that Deputy Reedus couldn't remember the plate numbers. Who in the world would remember the plate numbers? He remembered exquisite detail about the cars even without the shift report. They matched the description of the cars that Charlie Caswell had seen at the Allison house, including the fact that they were from Barlow County.

The jurors sat at their table and smoked their cigarettes and pipes and drank coffee and iced tea. They listened to the prosecutor and cleaned their fingernails, and smoked. When he had finished, the prosecutor asked them if they had any questions.

They stared at him. One juror asked if there were any other suspects in the case. The prosecutor told them there were not.

This grand jury had already heard several cases during their term so they already had a foreman. The prosecutor told them he would leave the room and they could take as long as they wanted to deliberate. He said there would be a deputy outside their door and when they reached a decision or had any questions they should knock on the door and the deputy would come to the prosecutor's temporary office in the courthouse and get him.

The prosecutor and his investigator walked down the hall to take the stairs to their office. The deputy called the prosecutor before they reached the top of the stairs. They headed back to the jury room. The foreman reported that they had unanimously voted for a True Bill. The all white grand jury had indicted Dr. Arnold Fulton for an offense against a Negro. This was a first.

# JEREMY BROOKS

Jeremy Brooks had spent his adult life practicing law. Fresh out of law school he had clerked for old Will Upchurch for a pittance while studying for the bar exam, earning barely enough for room and board at Miss Ida Hampton's boarding house, and a cup of coffee every morning at Jack's Cafe.

Of course he could drink coffee all day long at the law office, and did, but that was just drinking coffee. Jeremy needed to get out of the office some just to socialize and see people being people. And with his aspirations to hang up his own shingle once he was admitted to the bar, he needed for people to see him. He had grown up on the mountain, and just about everybody there knew him but the problem was that they knew him as Jeremy Brooks, one of the kids that had grown up among them.

In our jurisdiction young lawyers could start practicing law and even handling cases in court before they passed the bar examination as long as they did so under the tutelage and supervision of an honorable member of the bar, a species of which our town had several. Blessed with a rather large number of practicing lawyers, our town had become perhaps more litigious than other towns its size, and over the years lawsuits had become a form of entertainment that was enjoyed by litigants and courtroom observers alike. The lawyers had sense enough to keep their fees low so people could afford to litigate frequently and keep the lawyers busy.

So it was that Jeremy had been able to get into the trenches and try several cases from start to finish before he was ever admitted to the bar, and the best part was that he had won most of them. He was smart, articulate, and learned in the law, and above all he knew how to talk about the substance of his cases. He knew that if a farmer paid his neighbor in advance a breeding fee for use of the neighbor's bull, and the cow didn't take even after three or four attempts, then the only right thing to do was for the owner of the bull to give the man his money back. But even better than all this, and what made Jeremy Brooks begin to stand out as a good lawyer, was that he knew that everybody else knew what the result should be, even the owner of the bull, and so nobody was mad when he won. On the contrary, everybody went home relatively satisfied, but more importantly entertained, even the loser, who was out only a dollar for court costs – he knew the breeding fee didn't rightly belong to him anyway – and three or four dollars for his lawyer. It was worth a few dollars to him to find out who the better lawyer was. Next time Jeremy Brooks would be his lawyer. The owner of the cow which couldn't or wouldn't couple properly got his money back, less three dollars that he had to pay the lawyer for the trial, but he left the courtroom a winner walking beside the best young lawyer on the mountain in full view of a courtroom packed full of people. Walking out as the victor was certainly worth three dollars in itself. Everybody was happy, Jack's was packed for lunch, and the two litigants enjoyed their meals at tables not three feet apart. Life was good.

And so people began to call on Jeremy Brooks to handle their cases. He passed the bar and hung up his shingle with the blessing of Will Upchurch, who was old and rich and ready to retire. Will had been a good lawyer, somewhat of an academic who actually loved to read law. Over the years he had acquired a remarkable law library, which he gave to Jeremy Brooks when he retired, shortly after Jeremy opened his own office. Jeremy, too, loved to read law and this resulted in his prevailing from time to time when the issues presented a real legal challenge. Thus it was that even as a young lawyer, he had begun to develop a reputation as both a scholarly and practical lawyer.

Jeremy practiced law for ten years handling every kind of case except land boundary disputes, which could get somebody killed, and divorces, of which there were very few, and which also could get somebody killed. He honed his skills trying criminal cases on the mountain and in surrounding counties and continued to build a name for himself. By the time the Fulton case came up, Jeremy Brooks was considered by many to be the best criminal defense lawyer in the state.

Jeremy had been in the same high school graduating class as Arnold Fulton, III. They had been casual friends throughout their childhood, hunting and fishing together occasionally, and playing baseball and basketball together on the high school teams. Jeremy's family were not rich like the Fultons, but they were solid. Jeremy's father owned one of the two hardware stores in town and made a decent living supplying the farmers and builders and practically everybody else on the mountain. If Jeremy needed something for school he got it, just as Arnold did. The boys themselves didn't notice any difference in their social status and they thoroughly liked each other. Jeremy was a bit the smarter one. When he graduated from high school he got a full scholarship to Chapel Hill and continued his studies there through law school.

Arnold sought Jeremy's counsel when he was indicted and after some discussion Jeremy agreed to defend Arnold. He reviewed all the documents in the criminal file and talked to all the witnesses who had testified in the grand jury proceedings. He had some misgivings about the representation because he believed that Burt Reedus was an honest man, and he believed him when he said that he had seen two Barlow County cars in front of Arnold's house the night of the assault. He also knew Charlie Caswell and knew that he was an honest man. But he loved the law and the legal system, and he understood the function of lawyers, and he knew that he could and would be clinical in his representation and give Arnold the best defense available. He had learned years before that whether or not his client had committed the crime had nothing to do with the quality of the representation to which he was entitled. He would do everything he could within the law and the canons of ethics to get Arnold acquitted.

# THE TRIAL

The courtroom was packed and noisy. The white people and the Cherokee people sat and stood in the main seating area downstairs, and the Negroes filled the balcony which was the only place they were allowed in the courtroom unless one or more of them was sitting at the defense table as a defendant.

Dr. Arnold Fulton III had just taken a seat at the defense table. He had been allowed to enter by a side door that connected the administrative offices of the courthouse with the courtroom. When he came through the door the courtroom became quiet except for an occasional There he is and Who woulda ever thought it?

The jury pool was brought in and the bailiffs seated them in the first four rows of the courtroom on both sides. Judge Steadings had offered to disqualify himself at the beginning of the proceedings to avoid any appearance of impropriety in the trial and had asked the state supreme court to assign a special judge for the trial. But both the prosecution and the defense had said that wasn't necessary so Judge Steadings stayed on the case.

"All rise!" yelled one of the bailiffs when the judge stepped from behind the panel that separated the bench and the judge's chambers. The judge sat and the bailiff again yelled "This court is now in session. God save these United States, this blessed state, and this honorable court. Be seated and let there be no noise or hats on in the courtroom!"

The show had begun. No one in the courtroom today could remember anyone of Arnold's stature ever having been tried in this courthouse, and the courtroom had never been this full. The judge spoke to the crowd.

"Ladies and gentlemen, we are here today to conduct a trial, and we're glad to have you all here. There's not going to be anything unusual about this trial except that I asked for a special prosecutor so there won't be any question in anyone's mind about this trial being conducted absolutely properly, in other words without any home cookin' as some of you would say. It's going to be conducted just like every other trial that takes place here. We're glad to have all you citizens here with us but let me warn you: there will be no emotional outbursts in the courtroom by anyone. We've got the windows open and the fans running but we all know that some of these September days can be the hottest of the year, so if any of you feel it bearing down on you too heavy and you feel like you've got the monkeys on your back, feel free to go outside and get some fresh air but do it quietly without creating any commotion. There will be no spitting on the floor – there's four spittoons along each side wall. If you're chewing or dipping try to sit close enough to the wall so you won't have to go so far to spit. And no cigarette butts on the floor. There's ash trays about every three feet on the back of the benches."

He turned to the clerk. "Any problems with the venire?"

"No Your Honor. Everybody came."

"Swear the jury pool."

The clerk told the forty-eight citizens who had been summoned for jury duty to stand and raise their right hands. They stood and raised their hands – seven or eight of them raised their left hands. "Right hands please," barked the clerk. These made the correction, but five of those who had raised their right hands the first time also corrected and now raised their left. Frustrated, the clerk turned to the judge.

"Swear'em," he muttered. "Looks like a fine venire – a quarter of'em cain't tell their left hand from their right."

"Do you solemnly swear or affirm that you will give true and complete answers to the questions put to you today by the court and the attorneys conducting this trial, so help you God?"

Forty-eight mouths uttered Yes or I do or something of the sort, and the jury pool was sworn.

During the next two hours the judge and the lawyers asked these prospective jurors questions about whether they knew anything about the case, whether they had any kind of bias that would prevent the defendant from getting a fair trial, whether they were in any way related to the defendant or the lawyers, whether they had ever received surgical services from Dr. Fulton.

Everybody knew about the case. A few said Arnold was the sorriest excuse for a human being that they had ever seen; the judge excused them for cause. A few said Arnold had operated on them. Three said that they had relatives who had died while Arnold was operating on them. His lawyer asked the judge to excuse them for cause. The judge asked those people if they could nevertheless give the defendant a fair trial and they said yes. The judge said he didn't think that was cause to excuse them since they had stated they had no bias. And so it went for two hours. They finally had fourteen people sitting in the jury box, twelve regulars plus two alternates. The lawyers now had an opportunity to exercise their peremptory challenges – they could strike any juror from the box for any reason or no reason. The defense had five challenges and the state had five. Jeremy struck the three who had relatives who had died on the operating table. The state struck three. The alternates moved into the regulars' seats and each side struck one more and then both sides declined to exercise any more challenges. The clerk called eight more jurors to replace those who had been stricken by peremptory challenge.

"Swear the jury!" the judge said. The clerk swore them.

The judge read some instructions to the jury for about twenty minutes and announced that the court would be taking the dinner break and that the trial would resume at one o'clock at which time the lawyers would make opening statements.

Back in court after the dinner break the prosecutor spoke to the jury and to a packed courtroom. He talked about Tammy Allison and what a promising young pianist she was before the assault and how her future as a musician had been ruined by the dastardly assault that had been committed upon her. He talked about motive. He told the jury – and the packed courtroom – that this was not a race issue but rather a matter of family pride gone rotten. He talked about how Dr. Arnold Fulton couldn't bear even the thought of his daughter being defeated in a piano competition and thus not being able to represent our town and our mountain in the regional semi-finals. He conceded that race may have played a part in the crime in that it may have been even more difficult for Dr. Fulton to see his daughter defeated, and soundly so, by a colored girl. He told the jury that there was no eye witness to this crime other than the men who had actually crushed Tammy's hand, and of course Tammy herself, and that it was so dark in her bedroom when she was attacked that she couldn't possibly have identified the attackers even if they were here in the courtroom. But there was, he said, sufficient circumstantial evidence to show that Dr. Arnold Fulton was behind the attack and had used others to do it for him. He said this made him just as guilty as the man who raised the piece of wood and slammed it down again and again on Tammy's hand, crushing it to a pulp. Finally, he told the jury that they would see photographs of Tammy's hand that were taken at the hospital the night of the attack, and they would see the bloodstained board that had been used as the instrument of the attack. The prosecutor ended by telling the jury that they must completely eliminate racial differences from their trial of this case and make their decision based solely upon the evidence – and he repeated it – the evidence presented here in open court.

Arnold Fulton sat quietly at the defense table, occasionally looking at the prosecutor and writing a note from time to time.

Jeremy Brooks rose and spoke to the jury.

"Gentlemen of the jury, thank you for your service here today. You may be surprised to hear me ask you to do the same thing that the prosecutor has just asked you to do. Yes indeed, Dr. Fulton and I ask you to make your decision based solely on the evidence that will be presented here in court during this trial. Dr. Fulton has pled not guilty to the charges against him and this means that under our system of law there is a presumption of innocence that must be accorded him and that you must find him not guilty unless the state overcomes that presumption of innocence by presenting conclusive proof beyond a reasonable doubt. The state will not be able to do that, gentlemen, because such proof does not exist. Oh, there'll be insinuations and innuendo and other forms of circumstantial evidence, but there will never be sufficient evidence presented in this court to enable you to conclude beyond a reasonable doubt that Dr. Fulton is guilty of the charges against him in this case.

"There will be testimony that one of the sheriff's deputies saw two cars from Barlow County parked on the street out in front of Dr. Fulton's home on the night of the attack. There will be testimony that someone saw two cars from Barlow County speeding away from Tammy Allison's home the night of the attack. Gentlemen, Barlow County is our neighbor! I would suggest to you that if we were to walk the streets of our city at this moment we would probably see several cars around town bearing Barlow County plates. The mere fact that there may have been a couple of Barlow County cars in front of Dr. Fulton's house that night will not be proof of anything.

"Gentlemen, Dr. Fulton and I didn't just fall off the turnip truck – we're not dumb. We know that probably more than half the mountain believes that Dr. Fulton hired somebody to carry out this terrible attack on this innocent young lady. All you have to do is go over to Jack's for your mid-morning coffee or to eat a bite at dinner time to hear what people are thinking. But that's precisely why we are here today – to test these views in a court of law. It's not a matter of what the people here on the mountain believe or suspect. It's rather a matter of what the state can prove using the system of jurisprudence that you and the rest of this court – including this judge and I – are sworn to uphold. It's a matter of you making a decision based on the evidence that is presented here during this trial rather than on your feelings or suspicions. Suspicions have no place in a jury room. I ask you to set aside all of the suspicions that you may have brought to this courthouse today and pay close attention to the evidence that will be presented and make your decision based on that evidence and nothing else. Thank you."

The judge thanked the lawyers for their statements and turned to the prosecutor. "Call your first witness."

The prosecutor called two deputies to establish the details of the sheriff's office investigation. He then called the night nurse who testified about the time that Tammy arrived at the hospital and what happened when she was brought in. Then he put on one of the deputies that the sheriff had sent to be with Dr. Allison when his daughter arrived at the emergency room. The deputy described Dr. Allison's reaction when he saw his daughter's hand. This deputy had taken pictures of her hand and the prosecutor showed the deputy the pictures and asked him if he recognized them.

"Yep, those are the pictures I took when the little girl was brought in that night."

"Do they accurately show what you saw when you took the pictures?"

"Yes they do. Her hand didn't even look like a human hand. If you look at these that's what you see – a bloody, mangled mess. It made me want to throw up when I first saw it."

There was a murmur in the courtroom.

Jeremy let that one go by. He didn't want to push the jury at this point.

Next was Mrs. Allison. She told about her husband receiving a call around midnight to go to the hospital for what appeared to be emergency surgery, and her being jumped by some men shortly after her husband left. She told of finding Tammy and seeing her mangled hand and going outside on the porch and screaming. She never saw the men's faces in the dim light inside the house.

To establish motive, the prosecutor then questioned her about the piano competition. Her daughter had won the competition and Louise Fulton had taken the runner-up award. This meant that Tammy would represent the town in the finals unless something prevented her from competing, in which case Louise would represent the town.

The prosecutor then called Charlie Caswell to the stand. He established where Charlie lived and the fact that he frequently took late night walks in both colored and white neighborhoods around town.

"Now Mr. Caswell, you stated a few moments ago that you often take walks late in the evening in Free Town and in the white neighborhoods. Did you take a late night walk the night that Tammy Allison got her hand crushed?"

"Yes sir."

"And where did you walk that night?"

"In the colored neighborhood several blocks from my house."

"Did you notice anything unusual during your walk that night?"

"Yes I did."

"What did you notice that was unusual?"

"I saw two cars from Barlow County parked on the street right in front of Dr. Allison's house."

"What was unusual about that?"

"Well, first of all, everybody in that neighborhood parks their car in their driveway. It's rare to see a car parked on the street, especially at that time of night. So I walked up to them and looked at their license plates. And the main thing is you just don't see cars from Barlow County parked in that neighborhood. I've been walking those streets for years and I've never seen one. Everybody knows there's not a single Negro living in Barlow County so I knew it wouldn't be Negroes visiting their kind in that neighborhood."

"Do you know what kind of cars they were?"

"No Sir. They were two dark colored sedans, but I wouldn't know what make they were."

"Are you sure both cars were from Barlow County?"

"Absolutely. It said Barlow on the plate and I wrote down the tag numbers of both cars."

"If it was dark how could you see to read the plate numbers?"

"It wasn't dark. It was a full moon in September and the night was crisp and dry. You know how they are. It was so bright you could see colors even at midnight."

The prosecutor stepped to the defense table and handed Jeremy a piece of paper. Jeremy nodded and handed it back. The prosecutor asked the judge if he could approach the witness, the judge nodded and the prosecutor handed Charlie the paper.

"Do you recognize this?"

"I do."

"What is it?"

"That's the paper that I wrote the numbers down on. There's the numbers right there." Charlie pointed to the paper.

The prosecutor turned to the judge. "The state moves for the admission of this exhibit Your Honor."

The judge looked at Jeremy.

"No objection Your Honor," said Jeremy.

"Admitted. That will be marked as State's exhibit one."

The prosecutor asked a few more questions, establishing that Charlie had seen four men running out of Dr. Allison's house but couldn't see their faces and that he had seen the two cars speed away. Charlie also testified that moments after the cars sped away, he heard screams coming from Dr. Allison's place and he ran up to the porch where Mrs. Allison was standing on the front porch, still screaming.

Jeremy followed his instincts and declined to cross-examine Charlie. He didn't see any benefit that could be derived from cross-examining Charlie, and there was always a possibility that some harm could come from it. On balance it made sense to move on without questioning this witness.

The prosecutor called deputy Burt Reedus next. The clerk swore him in and Burt took a seat in the witness box.

The prosecutor began by asking some questions about Burt himself, and everybody in the courtroom, jury included, already knew the answers to these questions. He then asked Burt about the night of the crime.

"Do you remember where you were during the evening hours of the night that Miss Allison was attacked?"

"Yes Sir – I was pretty much all over town. I've been on night duty for the last couple of years. I work the four to twelve shift."

"Do you remember anything unusual about your work that evening?"

"Yes Sir, I do."

"Tell the court what you remember."

"Well, as I do every night, I drove around town checking out the neighborhoods, making sure everything was peaceful."

"Was it?"

"Yes Sir, but I did notice something unusual. I saw two cars with Barlow County tags parked in front of Dr. Fulton's house."

"Well, what was so unusual about that?"

"Well, Sir, I've been driving by Dr. Fulton's house every night I'm on duty for the last two years, and I've never seen a car from Barlow County parked in front of his house before."

"Did you do anything about this unusual occurrence Deputy Reedus?"

"Not really. It's not illegal for people from Barlow County to drive their cars over here and park them on the streets. But I did write down the license plate numbers and I put them in my shift report in a note about the cars being parked there. I also noted in the report that they were Fords."

"Do you remember those license plate numbers?"

"No Sir."

"Do you have the shift report?"

"No Sir."

"What happened to it?"

"I don't know. I wrote it up and put it in a manila folder and put it on the sheriff's desk like I do every night – but it disappeared. We've looked high and low all over that office for the report several times, and it's nowhere to be found. The sheriff told me it wasn't in the folder, but I know I put it there."

"Do you remember what the cars looked like?"

"Yes Sir. They were both dark Ford Sedans, late thirties, black I believe, although I couldn't swear to it. It was already close to midnight when I saw'em."

"Was there a street light there?"

"No Sir, but there was a full moon and it was plenty light enough to read the license plate, but it was not light enough so I could swear the cars were black, dark blue, dark green or whatever."

"I understand."

The prosecutor turned to the judge. "I pass the witness."

"Mr. Brooks, you may cross-examine." The judge didn't seem very interested.

Jeremy asked Burt a few innocuous questions and sat down. The prosecution really hadn't done any damage, and because he had received full discovery in the case – notice of all the evidence that the other side had against his client – he knew they didn't have any strong evidence, and frankly thought that the prosecutor was grabbing at straws in bringing the case to trial. Even if his client was guilty, the evidence just wasn't there to prove it. And under the American system of jurisprudence you have to prove it – probably just doesn't work.

The prosecutor then called the Barlow County Clerk to the stand and established that the two license plate numbers that Charlie Caswell had written down were assigned to two black Ford Sedans in her county.

"You could identify the owners of the vehicles through your records, correct?"

"Yes Sir."

"And did you do that?"

"Yes Sir. One of them belonged to one of our school teachers, and the other one belonged to Zeb Langston. He owns Langston's Hardware. Both of them were reported stolen the day after ya'll's trouble over here. I checked my records 'cause our sheriff always checks with our office when a car is reported stolen just to make sure everything matches up. I put a note about it in my office journal right after the sheriff called."

The prosecutor thanked the witness and passed her to the defense for cross-examination. "No questions, Your Honor," said Jeremy.

"Call your next witness." The judge appeared to be perturbed.

The prosecutor asked the court for a moment to confer with those at his table.

That was it. The state had established motive, and two very credible witnesses had testified that on the night Tammy Allison was attacked, one of them had seen two dark colored Ford sedans from Barlow County in front of Dr. Fulton's house and the other had seen two dark colored sedans from Barlow County in front of Dr. Allison's house. The witness who had been near Dr. Allison's house also provided Barlow County license plate numbers for the two vehicles and had testified that he had seen them speeding away from Dr. Allison's house. He had seen four men running out of the house but he had not been able to see their faces. Based upon the Barlow County clerk's testimony, it was clear that the owners of the vehicles had nothing to do with the attack.

But that was it.

The prosecutor turned to the judge. "The state rests, Your Honor."

"Counsel in chambers!" barked the judge.

———◆———

"What are you going to do Jeremy?" The judge was clearly perturbed now.

"When we go back out there I am going to consult with my client, and if he agrees with my counsel, we're not going to put on a defense. They haven't proven anything. No reasonable jury could conclude beyond a reasonable doubt that Arnold Fulton committed the charged offense just because two Ford sedans from Barlow County were seen at his house and two Ford sedans from Barlow County were seen at the Allison's the night of the attack. It would be a completely different story if we had matching license plates, but we don't."

Judge Steadings turned to the prosecutor. "Is that really all you have? You know as well as I do there's not enough of a nexus there between the cars at the Fultons' place and the cars at the Allisons' place."

The prosecutor was silent for a moment. "Judge, I wish I had more, but that's it. Everybody on the mountain knows he did it, but I'm afraid that's all I can do regarding proof."

"You'd clearly have something if you had the same license plates at both places, especially since they were stolen, but you don't have that. I just don't see how a rational trier of fact can conclude beyond a reasonable doubt that Arnold committed this heinous act just because of those two cars parked in front of his house, and I doubt that you do either."

The prosecutor looked at the judge and said nothing.

The judge turned to Jeremy. "Well?"

"I'll be asking for a directed verdict."

"You won't get it. I'm not going to take the heat on this one, Jeremy. I'll deny it and if you decide not to put on a case, I'll let the jury make the first decision. Maybe they'll do what they're supposed to and acquit him. If they don't, I'm sure you'll fire up a motion for JNOV before I can blink twice."

Judges rarely granted motions for a judgment *non obstante veredicto,* or notwithstanding the verdict, especially in criminal cases. But good judges would do it when it was required by the interests of justice. This happened sometimes when a jury would come back with a guilty verdict when the proof was clearly not there at all. Motions for directed verdict, cases where the judge acquitted the defendant without even allowing the jury to make the decision, were even more rare because the judge could avoid public wrath by shifting it to the jury in those rare cases where they were willing to acquit in a case where the whole world wanted a guilty verdict.

"Let's see where this goes." The judge stood and the three men walked back into the courtroom.

———◆———

Jeremy rose and addressed the court.

"Your Honor, I respectfully ask this court to direct a verdict of not guilty in this case. The state has not put on one iota of proof that my client committed this offense. The fact that two Ford sedans from Barlow County were parked in front of my client's house the same night that two Ford sedans from Barlow County were parked in front of Dr. Allison's house proves nothing, especially since there is absolutely no proof whatsoever that they were the *same* two Ford sedans. Cars from Barlow County travel our county roads and city streets daily I'm sure Your Honor. They often park on our streets and I'm sure that quite a number of them are Ford sedans. Your honor, the court should direct the jury to return a verdict of not guilty, and I ask it to do so."

The judge sat quietly for a few moments and then announced a brief recess. Fifteen minutes later he stepped back to his seat at the bench.

"I'll deny the motion, Mr. Brooks. You may proceed."

"Your Honor, Dr. Fulton and I agree that we need not put on a case. The state has utterly failed to put on any proof that my client committed this offense. There's not even any circumstantial evidence that he committed the offense."

The judge interrupted. "You can present your arguments later Mr. Brooks. What are you going to do?"

"The defense rests Your Honor."

The judge turned to the jury. "Gentlemen, Mr. Brooks

and his client have decided not to put on any proof. So here's what we're going to do. It's almost noon, so we'll take our dinner break now and come back at one-thirty at which time I will allow the lawyers to present their closing arguments and then I will give you instructions on the law that applies in this case. After that you will begin your deliberations and you can take as long as you need. We won't be in any hurry at all. I want you to take all the time you need to reach a proper verdict in this case. Any questions?"

The jury had no questions. The judge turned to the lawyers.

"Anything further from the lawyers at this time?"

They were ready to go to lunch. The judge stood.

"We'll be in recess until one-thirty."

———◆———

The jury had been out for about two hours. The lawyers went to Jack's and drank coffee. People milled about in the courtroom, smoking, talking, spitting, playing cards. The lawyers had put on a fine performance and the judge had read the law to the jurors and had sternly admonished them to follow it and had then sent them into the jury room to begin their deliberations.

The court deputy guarding the door to the jury room jumped up and opened the door.

"You knocked?"

Someone passed him a note. He took it to the judge. The judge read it and said to the deputy, "Call everybody back in. They've reached a verdict."

With the jury and the audience back in the courtroom, Judge Steadings took the bench and asked the jury if it had reached a verdict. When the jury foreman told him they had, the judge asked him to pass the verdict form to the bench. The deputy handed the form to the judge, the judge read it and then passed it back to the foreman of the jury.

"Ladies and gentleman, in a moment I will ask the jury

foreman to read the verdict to the court. I want to warn you that there must be no show of emotion when the verdict is read. This is a court of law and we will maintain order in this courtroom."

The courtroom was hushed.

"Mr. Foreman, what is your verdict?"

The foreman stood.

"We find the defendant guilty as charged."

There was a murmur of approval, but nobody yelled or applauded, at least not yet.

Arnold Fulton stared straight ahead, and said nothing. Jeremy leaned toward him and said, "He'll send everyone home now and call us back for post-trial motions tomorrow morning. He'll leave you free on bail tonight, and we'll present our motion tomorrow morning. The judge won't sleep a wink tonight, I assure you."

———◆———

Jeremy was right. The judge tossed fretfully all night. He knew what Jeremy was going to do in the morning, and he knew what he had to do as a judge who took his oath seriously. The mere fact that there were two cars from Barlow County parked in front of Arnold's house the same evening that Tammy Allison was attacked was simply not enough to sustain a conviction. There was just no evidence that the two cars in front of Arnold's house were the same two cars that were in front of Tammy Allison's house a little later. Everybody on the mountain knew they were, at least in the way of knowing that was accepted by everybody on the mountain, but that way of knowing is not acceptable in a criminal proceeding. Under the Constitution and the common law, conclusions in such proceedings are and should be held to a much higher standard. The jury had found Arnold guilty based on their passion rather than on the evidence. Unfortunately, that could not be allowed to stand.

The judge's problem was that now the mountain's wrath

would be on him; if the jury had found Arnold not guilty, then they would have had to take the heat. But now he was going to have to reverse their verdict and enter a new verdict of not guilty. Everybody on the mountain would hate him. He would never be re-elected to this judgeship. Oh well, he could practice law, or could he? Who here on the mountain would ever hire him as their lawyer? He would be an outcast in his own land. He kept tossing and turning, drifting in and out of sleep.

——◆——

The next morning the judge and the lawyers and Dr. Fulton were back in court. The courtroom was otherwise almost empty – much of the public had spent the remaining part of the afternoon and the evening celebrating Arnold's guilty verdict. The Negroes were amazed that an all white jury had convicted one of their own for causing the assault on a colored person. Whites frequently caused Negroes to be assaulted, but no white person on this mountain had ever been convicted of assaulting a Negro. They were jubilant. The verdict pleased the Cherokee for essentially the same reason, although they were generally not given to celebration; they took life as it came, took care of their own without regard to public opinion, and went about their business. But overall there was an air of happiness and cheer on the mountain this autumn morning, even among the Cherokee; but this was not the case in the chambers of Judge Steadings; he prepared some notes and finally stood and walked into the courtroom to do what he knew he had to do.

——◆——

"Mr. Brooks, it's your show."

"Respectfully your honor, I have no doubt that the court would act on its own motion if I didn't present my motion, but I'll go ahead. The defense asks the court to enter a judg-

ment notwithstanding the verdict of the jury, and to enter its
own verdict of not guilty in the case against Dr. Arnold Fulton."

The judge looked down at the file in front of him for a
few moments. Jeremy and the prosecutor did the same. Finally the judge looked up.

"The motion is granted. The court finds the defendant
not guilty, and the court's verdict and judgment will be sub-
stituted for the verdict of the jury."

Arnold stared straight ahead. Jeremy had told him this
would happen.

"Because I know this is going to cause an uproar in our
community – among all three races that dwell on this mountain – I'm going to attempt to state clearly the reasons that
compel me to do this.

"In our system of justice a criminal conviction has to be
reasonable. The jury must find the defendant guilty beyond
a reasonable doubt. This means that it has to be based on
sound reasoning about the evidence that has been presented
and admitted in the trial of the case. It is clearly the law, and
has been for a very long time, that the jury may not consider
any out of court information in reaching its verdict. It must
consider only the evidence that was presented by the parties
during the trial. Moreover, our law requires the jurors to set
aside their passions – not an easy thing to do – and to deliver
a verdict based solely upon the evidence.

"In this case the court finds that a verdict of guilty beyond a reasonable doubt cannot be derived solely from the
evidence that was presented by the state. The prosecution
presented clear evidence that there were two cars from Barlow County parked in front of Dr. Allison's house at the time
of the assault. There was testimony by an eminently credible
witness that four men ran from the house right after the assault and that they sped away in those cars from Barlow
County. This witness testified that he had written down the
license plate numbers of the two cars and this evidence including the plate numbers was admitted by the court. There

was testimony by the Barlow County Clerk that the vehicles had been stolen on the date of the attack, so there can be no inference that the lawful owners of the vehicles had any accountability in the commission of this crime.

"There was also testimony by another eminently credible witness that there were two cars bearing Barlow County license plates parked in front of the defendant's house the same evening as the attack. The problem is that there is simply no evidence before the court to permit any juror to conclude, based on reason, that they are the same two cars in front of each place. Deputy Reedus testified that he saw the Barlow County cars in front of Dr. Fulton's house shortly before the attack, and that he wrote down their license plate numbers and noted them in his shift report. However, the shift report could not be located even after many diligent searches for it, and not surprisingly Deputy Reedus could not recall the license plate numbers when he testified at trial.

"If we had had testimony and other evidence that showed that the license plate numbers on the cars in front of Dr. Fulton's residence just moments before the attack were precisely the same as the license plate numbers of the cars in front of Dr. Allison's residence during the attack, then we would have strong circumstantial evidence that in the court's view could reasonably sustain a guilty verdict. We never reached the "click" point where the reasonable mind could say Yep, that's enough because they were the same two stolen cars, and he certainly had a motive. But we don't have that. We never reached the point where a reasonable mind could be in repose with a verdict of guilty.

"There has been an enormous amount of passion about this case over the last twelve months and frankly, the verdict is an historical one. For the first time in our jurisdiction a white jury has convicted a white citizen – a very prominent one nonetheless – of an offense against one of our Negro citizens. Based upon things I've been told over the last few hours, our broad community feels that racial justice is finally within reach here. But based upon the reasons I've stated, I have no choice but to set aside the jury's verdict and to enter a verdict of not guilty in the charge against Dr. Fulton."

The judge paused.

"Arnold Fulton is hereby acquitted. A judgment will enter."

The judge stood and stepped behind the panel and through the door to his chambers. Arnold smiled at the handful of people in the courtroom as he walked out. Jeremy remained seated at the defense table, still looking toward the bench, almost as if he could see through the wall into chambers. He knew that what had just occurred was one of those rare, outstanding events in the exercise of jurisprudence, and he knew without a doubt that he was in the presence of greatness.

# HOME AFTER THE TRIAL

**B**efore sunset of the day after the trial ended, or more particularly the day the judge set aside the jury's verdict of guilty and entered the court's verdict of not guilty, Arnold Fulton and his family left town for a two-week vacation. The judge adjourned court for the rest of the day and we went home. The judge was disgusted, and Mama just left him alone for the rest of the afternoon. He went into his study and we could hear him talking to himself and pacing around. He made several trips out to the garden and the pigpen, and each time came back to his study and paced around some more. Just before supper the sheriff drove up. He got out and came up to the porch and Mama met him at the door.

"Come in Sheriff."

"Don't mean to bother you at suppertime Mrs. Steadings but I'd like to talk with the judge for a few minutes if it's not too much of a bother."

"No bother at all, Sheriff. Supper's not done yet anyway and you'll sure be welcome to stay and have a bite with us."

"I sure appreciate that Ma'am but I've got some things I got to get right on as soon as I talk to the judge."

Mama showed the sheriff to Daddy's study. Daddy was in the garden so Mama went to the back door and yelled toward the garden.

The sheriff was waiting in the study. Daddy went in and left the door open, so we could all hear what was going on. I could even see them standing there.

"Judge, there's been a lot of commotion over in Nigger Town all afternoon. I'm afraid something's getting ready to bust over there."

"Sheriff, I'd appreciate it if you'd call that part of our city Free Town. That's part of our problem around here."

"Hell, Judge, half the niggers call it Nigger Town, but I'll try to work on that."

"Thank you. Now what do you want me to do?"

"I think you need to start calling some of your preachers over there and get'em to calm things down a little."

"What makes you think it's getting that bad?"

"Well I've never seen the colored section of the courtroom packed like it was for this trial, and I've never seen so many Cherokees in court, and I'd say right at a hundred per cent of them think Dr. Fulton is guilty."

"Well the court found him not guilty and legally that's that! It's over. Done."

"I understand that Judge, but as you know there's the law and then there's people. In a situation like this the people don't seem to hold the law in as high a regard as you and I do."

Daddy got a look on his face that I had seen before like he was getting ready to snap at somebody, but he just glanced aside and then back at the sheriff.

"Alright. I'll talk to a few people. But let me suggest you keep your patrols out of Free Town tonight and the next few days. There's not a thing they can do over there that will help the situation, and there's probably a lot they could do that would just start some trouble."

"Sure enough Judge. Just so you'll know, Dr. Fulton and his family are taking a coupla weeks vacation. You might want to let them know that. And I'm gonna try to take a few days off here in the next week or so and go down to the coast for a few days of fishing. Burt'll be able to handle things while I'm gone."

"Thank you Sheriff."

As the sheriff left the room Daddy got that disgusted look on his face again and stomped out the back door and went back to his garden and the pigpen until Mama called us to supper a half hour later. Obviously still disgusted, Daddy ate fast and said nothing during the meal. As soon as he finished he got up from the table and headed toward the door.

"I'm going to see if Charlie's home. I'll be back in a few minutes. I need to talk to somebody around here that's got some common sense."

Mama smiled at him as he left.

———◆———

The judge and Charlie sat in rocking chairs on the front porch as they had many times before, and I sat in the porch swing. It had been hot in the courtroom but here on the porch there was a slight breeze. The sun was setting and the air was cooling. The evening should have been one of those pleasant, soft mountain evenings that we had so often in late summer, but it wasn't. The judge was tense, agitated. He rocked as Charlie spoke.

"You do need to call the preachers," Charlie said. "I don't think they're gonna riot, but they're getting noisy over there, and I saw a lot of Cherokee folk over there just before you came to the house to get me. That's something I don't see very much, a whole crowd of 'em there at the same time. If there's trouble the Cherokee'll side with the colored folk."

"I'll call 'em. I've never seen so many of the colored people in court, or Cherokee for that matter."

Earlier in the afternoon during one of the judge's conversations with himself (this was one of his traits – he carried on detailed, extensive conversations with himself regularly, working out whatever was vexing him), I had heard him talk about how he didn't think the colored people would do any harm to anyone but who knows what the Cherokee might do out of loyalty to their friends in Free Town. Everybody on the mountain knew that Arnold was guilty as sin. In the minds of the jurors there apparently was plenty of circumstantial evidence to convict him. The lack of the plate numbers from the shift report apparently didn't bother them and so they con-

victed Arnold even though Burt couldn't produce the plate
numbers of the cars from Barlow County. Charlie's note had
been entered into evidence and placed the cars at Dr. Allison's
house and showed the plate numbers and showed that both
cars were from Barlow County. Burt placed two Barlow
County cars at Arnold's house shortly before Charlie saw
them at Dr. Allison's house and he testified that he wrote
down the tag numbers and time, and put that information in
his patrol report. And the description of the cars matched. But
that was not enough to put his judicial mind at ease. It just
didn't do it.

But Jeremy Brooks had delivered a sound, compelling
defense argument, and although he did not convince the jury
that they shouldn't convict without that critical piece of evidence, the so-called shift report that would absolutely connect the two cars to both Arnold's house and Dr. Allison's
house by showing an exact match of the license tag numbers,
he certainly convinced the judge – or at least affirmed the
judge's own view – that it was legally impossible to allow a
guilty verdict to stand.

Everybody on the mountain knew that Arnold had done
it. Even the jurors knew Arnold had done it. That's why they
had found him guilty, but the judge knew that this kind of
knowledge was not based on reason but was rather grounded
in this deeper source of knowing, with which we are all in
contact, by which we all know, but which the legal system
does not, and cannot, sanction as a source for legal truth. Jeremy had emphasized that a conviction must be based on the
evidence presented in court, and the only evidence against
Arnold was Burt's testimony that he had seen two Barlow
County cars parked in front of Arnold's house earlier in the
evening and Charlie's testimony that the two cars he had seen
in front of the Allison house were from Barlow County. He
hadn't even called the sheriff as a defense witness to establish
that there was no report in the files that showed any Barlow
County tag numbers. Everybody on the mountain knew the
truth. But the more he thought about it, Jeremy was right.

The critical evidence just wasn't there. He understood the verdict. But it surely wouldn't have been upheld on appeal.

Daddy went over all of this again with Charlie there on the porch. Daddy talked and rocked and Charlie listened. The streetlights came on. They talked about Burt. Charlie and Burt were friends. Not as close as Charlie and Daddy but they spent time together and hunted and fished together. There was not a doubt in Charlie's or Daddy's mind that Burt had filed that report. They talked about the sheriff.

"That sheriff's rotten," Daddy said. He glanced at me when he said that but just kept rocking. "I've got a feeling most of the people on this mountain think the sheriff did something with that report."

Charlie rocked and slapped at a mosquito. "Why would he do that?"

"I don't know, but I aim to find out."

# ARNOLD FULTON
## AFTER THE TRIAL

Arnold accepted the fact that most people on the mountain thought that he was guilty, and that the jury was correct in its verdict, but he was secure now because he had been acquitted by the court notwithstanding the jury's verdict and he could never be retried on those charges. Jeremy had explained to him in detail the protections of the Double Jeopardy Clause when they met to conclude Jeremy's representation in the matter. He didn't care about people thinking he was guilty because he was convinced that those people didn't care either. His view was that he was protected by the system and that he was now safe. He was simply not capable of understanding that even the normally racist white people on the mountain have limits on the amount of evil that they are willing to accept. His view was that though Tammy Allison was the daughter of the only nigger surgeon in town, who was one of only four surgeons on the mountain, she was still a nigger and the people who were convinced that he was responsible for what had happened to her just would not ever consider her to be as important as him. Niggers were niggers and that was that. He was a white surgeon, the only real surgeon on the mountain – the other two white surgeons were both old drunks – everybody on the mountain needed him just as much as they had needed his father. There was not a white person on the mountain that would choose the nigger surgeon's services over his. It just wouldn't happen, not on this mountain. The only white people that used the nigger's services were unconscious when they arrived at the hospital or were in such pain that they were out of their minds.

And there were those who were so poor they couldn't afford Arnold and had no property to support credit with him so they did not get the credit or the surgical services even when he was their healer of choice. In Arnold's view these people might as well have been niggers so they didn't matter to him at all. He didn't care what they thought. He knew that he would still get most of the surgical business on the mountain from the whites that mattered. He was thus secure in his ability to earn a good living on the mountain even if people knew deep down what had really happened to Tammy Allison.

And Arnold knew he had a steadfast ally in Sam Bartlett. He knew that he couldn't be tried on the same charges again but his arrangement with Sam gave him added comfort. Their complicity was oddly satisfying to Arnold. He wondered if the sheriff understood that he had bound himself to Arnold with this minor extortion by making himself vulnerable to exposure and that they would be a team here on this mountain until one of them died. This gave Arnold a feeling of intense satisfaction. In his view he now had control of law enforcement on the mountain. Circumstance had forced him into a partnership, even a kinship, with a very powerful man, and Arnold was enjoying it. In a few hours they would leave town for a couple of weeks to let things calm down, and when he returned he would enjoy his new power.

He stood and walked over to his liquor cabinet. He chose a jar of mountain whiskey that he kept in the back corner of the cabinet that he knew to be at least twenty years old. His father had given it to him years ago. Arnold was elated. He poured himself a tall glass of the nectar and drank deeply. He drank until he felt the peace that only the powerful can feel.

# THE SHIFT REPORT

Eight days following the trial Burt Reedus sat at his desk in the sheriff's office at about 10:30 in the evening and reviewed copies of the papers that he had served on various people during the early hours of his evening shift. He would frequently serve court papers in the evening simply because he could find people at home more easily then. When he served a paper, he left a copy with the person being served and brought a copy back to the office and stamped it with a rubber stamp and signed it. The next morning one of the day deputies would take the stamped and signed copy to the court clerk who would file it in the appropriate court file.

After reviewing the papers Burt reached for the rubber stamp which he kept on a stand next to his desk, but it was not there. He opened the middle drawer of his desk and looked; it was not there.

It occurred to him that the sheriff may have used it. He stood and walked over to the sheriff's desk and saw that the stamp was not there either. Then he opened the middle drawer of the sheriff's desk and there it was. When he reached for it he saw an envelope next to it with his name, Burt Reedus, written on it in the sheriff's handwriting. Curious, he took the envelope and looked more closely. He held it up to the light. He could see a paper with handwriting on it, and it looked like his handwriting. The envelope was not sealed. He hesitated for a moment, then pulled out the sheet of paper and unfolded it.

Burt was stunned. It was the carbon copy of the shift report! It was his handwriting and there were the license plate numbers of the Barlow County tags that he had included in the report when he had seen the two cars parked in front of Dr. Fulton's house the night Tammy Allison was assaulted. He was almost positive that they were the same numbers that Charlie Caswell had testified that he had written down when he saw the two Barlow County cars in front of Dr. Allison's house that night, but he would need to verify this. Charlie's note with the plate numbers on it would still be in the court file so he would be able to check this tomorrow as soon as the clerk of court opened her office and he could get his hands on the file. But he already knew.

What he didn't know was precisely why the sheriff had done this. Could it be because he simply wasn't going to allow a white surgeon to be convicted for cracking up a Negro girl's hand? That would be perfectly consistent with the sheriff's attitude toward Negroes. Or could it be that the sheriff saw an opportunity to help himself in some way by making the report disappear? He needed to talk to the judge about this. But not tonight. He would go by Charlie Caswell's house after the morning shift deputy arrived at midnight and leave this copy with Charlie.

Although it was rarely used, the sheriff's office had a 35 mm camera that they used to take crime scene pictures. Burt put a new roll of film in the camera and took several pictures of the shift report and the envelope and then removed the film, put in a new roll of film, and repeated the process. He would keep the film at his house until he could get it developed – which he would have done a couple of counties away so that no one would know about this for now – and he would have Charlie take the envelope to the judge in the morning. He reloaded the camera.

Dr. Fulton wasn't expected back for another week. The sheriff had left just yesterday to go to the coast and fish and drink for five days and wouldn't be back until the weekend. This would give Burt time to do what he needed to do without feeling that he had to hide his every move. It was not at all unusual for Burt to be at the courthouse during the day so nobody would think anything about it even though everybody knew he worked the evening shift. He needed to make sure that the case file in the courthouse did not disappear, or if it did disappear that there was a photographic copy of the paper from Charlie's notepad where he had written the license plate numbers of the Barlow County cars. He had heard the sheriff claim that there was a photograph of that piece of evidence in his safe, but he put no stock in that claim. It was the practice of the court to keep documents that had been entered into evidence during a trial in an envelope bound into the case file itself, so assuming that no one had removed it from the court file he should be able to locate it in the morning. He wrote down the plate numbers that were in the shift report and then put the shift report and the envelope in which he had found it into a larger manila envelope with the sheriff's office address printed on it. He sealed the larger envelope and drove straight to Charlie Caswell's place when the deputy arrived at midnight.

The clerk's office opened at 7:30. Burt was there with the camera when the clerk unlocked the door. He went straight to the shelves where the case files were kept, checked the clerk's index of cases, and pulled the file. He took it to a little back room where the lawyers and others could review files. After a moment of flipping through the different sections of the file, he found the envelope that he was looking for and removed its contents. He looked at the license plate numbers that he had written down and very carefully compared them to the ones that were on Charlie's note. Bingo! He moved the file to the end of the table next to a window and took several pictures of the envelope and the notepad paper. He now had clear proof that Arnold Fulton was guilty. Now they could get him.

———◆———

I had been knocking at Charlie's door for a full minute. This was unusual – Charlie normally got up when the roosters started crowing. Finally I heard him holler to come on in. I opened the door and stepped in – there were very few locked doors here on the mountain.

When I heard his back door open and close I sat in one of the chairs by the bookshelf and began leafing through a book; he was headed to the outhouse.

A few minutes later he came in and walked to his sink and turned on the cold water; he scrubbed his hands with lye soap and splashed water on his face and neck and wet his hair and slicked it back.

"I just came by to say hello. Sorry to get you out of bed so late in the morning."

He grinned. "Yeah I kinda slept in a little didn't I? Looks like it's already a little past seven. Yont some breakfast?"

"Naw, I ate an hour ago – you go ahead. I'll have a cup of coffee."

"Burt Reedus come by here about midnight. We visited for awhile and he left a paper with me. That's why I'uz still in bed when you got here. I had trouble gettin' back to sleep."

"What kind of paper?"

"I don't know but he said it had something to do with Arnold Fulton. He told me to make sure I got it to the judge this morning."

"You want me to take it to him?"

"That would be fine if you make sure he gets it. He said it was extremely important."

"I will."

He went to his back room and came back with a large brown envelope that had the sheriff's name and department address printed on it, and handed it to me. The envelope was sealed.

"I've never seen Burt as excited as he was last night. He wouldn't tell me what it was all about, but he said things were gonna change here on the mountain real fast and he told me to be extra careful for awhile until we get all this mess straightened out."

He made the coffee first and I drank my coffee while he

fried his eggs and his side meat. He sat down and ate his side meat and eggs and we drank coffee and chatted for a few more minutes, after which I took the envelope and went back home. I was beginning to get excited myself.

Daddy was still at the house when I got there and I gave him the envelope and told him what Charlie had told me about Burt being so excited. At the time I didn't know much about Burt Reedus, but I knew who he was and the story about how he had become a deputy. And I knew that Daddy had a lot of respect for him. When I told Daddy Burt had given the envelope to Charlie for Charlie to give to him, he perked up and got very interested. He opened the big envelope and removed the smaller unsealed envelope that was inside. He recognized the sheriff's handwriting on the unsealed envelope where the name Burt Reedus had been written. He had seen his handwriting many times over the years for one reason or another and he was satisfied that this was clearly the sheriff's handwriting. He pulled the carbon copy of the shift report from the envelope and began reading.

———————◆———————

I've rarely seen the judge so excited. When he finished reading the shift report he jumped up and grabbed his coat and hat and almost ran to the car. I ran with him and he didn't seem to object. We drove straight to the courthouse and he parked and went directly to the clerk's office and pulled Dr. Fulton's case file. He walked down the hall, walked past his secretary's desk and nodded at her, stepped into his office, let me slip past him, and slammed the door. He removed the evidence envelope from the file and compared the license plate numbers to those in the shift report. Then he called the sheriff's office and told the day deputy to leave Burt a note to come by our house when he came on duty that evening.

———————◆———————

Burt and Daddy sat in the study. Both of them had compared the plate numbers in the report with the ones in the case file. I was in the next room, which was a little sitting room where I did my homework.

"Okay, tell me where you found the report."

"It was right in the sheriff's desk, in the middle drawer. I couldn't find my rubber stamp on my desk or on the stand where I normally keep it, so I looked on the sheriff's desk. I didn't see it there either so I looked through his desk drawers. The stamp was there in his middle drawer and so was this envelope with my name on it."

"And you opened it."

"Not really. The envelope wasn't sealed. But yes, I was curious and I held it up to the light and saw my handwriting inside so I decided to pull it out and see what it was."

"Good."

"It was my shift report, and I figured I better get it to somewhere safe. I didn't want to wake you up at midnight so I took it over to Charlie and told him to get it over here to you first thing this mornin'. So there you are."

"All right. You did the right thing. But let me tell you, Burt, we better get ready for trouble. I need to think this through and then I'll talk to you some more about it. Let's keep this under wraps for now. By all means don't mention it to the sheriff if he calls from the coast."

The next morning the judge went to his office a little early and after his first cup of coffee he walked downstairs to the Register of Deeds. He had tossed and turned the night before trying to figure out why the sheriff might have caused the report to disappear. Of course it could have simply got lost, and then been found in the office by someone, but he didn't believe that had happened. The sheriff's staff had searched for it very carefully too many times. The fact was it was found in the sheriff's desk. The sheriff must have had something to do with it. Other than downright meanness – which was certainly not out of the question – the only thing the judge could figure was that the sheriff must have had some pecuniary interest in making the report disappear. He decided to check the public records to see if they showed any recent major purchases by the sheriff.

He checked the property transfer index. There was nothing there in the sheriff's name for this year other than some properties that had been foreclosed and sold in a sheriff's sale. But there was a piece of property on Swenson Road that had been deeded to Sam Bartlett last year. The judge wrote down the book and page number of the recorded deed and went into the records room and pulled the book. He found the page and saw that a two hundred thirty acre farm had been transferred to Sam Bartlett in fee simple by Blue Mountain Farms, a registered partnership, and based on his memory of the trial the judge was almost sure that the date on the deed was two or three days after Tammy Allison was attacked. When he finished here he would pull the court file from the trial to confirm that. He looked at the second page to see who had signed the deed as the grantor. There it was: Blair Fulton, Partner. Arnold had been smart and careful. He had created a small degree of deniability by having Blair sign the deed. He would check the partnership register to confirm that Blair and Arnold were the members of this partnership, and that Blair was authorized to act for the partnership, but he already knew what he would find.

The story was becoming clear: the sheriff had blackmailed Arnold. Burt had in fact put the shift report in the sheriff's in-box, just as he had testified, and the sheriff had reviewed it that morning and had removed the original and the carbon copy from the office. He had given Arnold the original and Arnold had given him the Swenson Farm. The sheriff had kept the copy for who knows what sinister use in the future – probably for more blackmail. Somehow months later he had absentmindedly tossed it into his desk, and now the truth was out.

The judge started to feel sick. It could not possibly be this simple. He went back to the index room and pulled the index to the deeds of trust, what some people called mortgages.

There it was. The public record showed that Sam Bartlett had signed a note to Blue Mountain farms for ninety percent of the sale price of the farm and had signed a deed of trust back to the partnership to secure the note. They had made the transaction look like a normal purchase. Although the whole thing stunk, as long as Sam and Arnold stuck to their story, it would be impossible to prove obstruction of justice or tampering with evidence, and he couldn't be retried on the original charge because of double jeopardy. They were perfectly covered. All the sheriff had to do was claim that he had finally found the copy of the shift report in the back of his desk drawer, and stick with that claim. He could even claim that he had written Burt's name on the envelope to be sure that Burt got his copy of the shift report. He could still claim that the original was lost and that he had no idea where it was. Given the current state of the facts and the sheriff's year-long denial that he had ever seen the shift report, as long as he and Arnold stuck by their stories there would be no way to implicate the sheriff in the disappearance of the report. And Arnold wouldn't expose the sheriff because if he did he would be subjecting himself to a charge of obstruction of justice.

But the judge knew this was not the worst part. What he faced now was a social eruption. When this came out, and it would come out, the people would demand that Arnold be retried, and the judge was going to have to try to explain to the Negroes and the Cherokee, and even the white people on the mountain, what the Double Jeopardy Clause of the United States Constitution was all about. The average person simply could not understand why a man who had already been tried and acquitted, even by a JNOV, could not be retried for the same crime even if after the acquittal there was solid proof that surfaced that he had committed the crime. And this was excellent proof. This was one of those cases where there was simply no remedy in the legal system for the wrong that had been committed. The judge understood the historical reasons for the double jeopardy protection, but in some cases the popular wisdom was completely

counter to these reasons. The whole mountain would be
ready to kill when he tried to explain that Arnold couldn't be
tried again. The whites had finally convicted one of their
own for committing a crime against a Negro, and now he,
their judge, had reversed the conviction. That was bad
enough. But now the whole mountain would be convinced
that he was protecting Arnold, and he would be blamed for
the trouble that he knew was coming.

The judge replaced the books and walked back upstairs
to his office and told his secretary to cancel all his appointments for the rest of the day. He was sick and disgusted – as
sick and disgusted as he had ever felt in his life. As he almost
always did when he felt greatly burdened he would go home
and get into his work clothes and work in his garden some,
and mess with his pigs and his steer. Never in his life had he
felt such an ominous feeling of impending disaster. The people that lived here on the mountain were mostly good people, but like men everywhere they could be pushed only so
far. The Cherokee who had dug up the courthouse lawn to
cook their pigs were digging up land that was theirs before
the white man took it from them, stole it from them. With
their barbeque they were symbolically declaring This is still
our land. They were rooted here like the Jews were rooted in
the Holy Land – when they arrived they may have displaced
a current people, but that was in the dim past. They had
managed to live in the present and to look to the future, and
certainly to protect themselves as witnessed by a number of
busted kneecaps and shattered shin bones among the white
population. And the Negroes were rooted here because the
white man had planted them here. Up to now they had been
relatively docile because they had been subdued and their
spirits had been suppressed by the white man, but they had
still put their faith in the system of justice that had been
promised them but which had rarely been delivered. And
the white man was here because he had left the motherland
– or been kicked out of it as an alternative to a public hanging – and he came and took the mountain, and kept it. He

imposed his culture and his law, and the Cherokee and the Negroes yielded to it, always in the hope that the promises would be fulfilled. But the white man broke them and promised again, and then rebroke them and repromised. And always the promises were broken. It had taken a civil war to change the Negroes from property to people, and they were promised justice, but that promise was broken. But in the law it had been done and they had become persons, and for decades now these three – the Cherokee, the Negroes, and the white man – had made their peace of sorts, and were still making progress at this peace, but this thing that had happened here on the mountain, or was about to happen, now, would bring that slow, deliberate movement toward social justice and equality to a halt. There had to be a way to handle this, to prevent a local civil war here on the mountain.

He called Burt over to his house as soon as he came on duty to try to explain the problem to him. He told him about the sheriff and the farm, and he explained his view that as long as the sheriff didn't make any missteps and as long as Arnold and the sheriff covered each other there wouldn't be any evidence that would support any charges against them for obstruction of justice. Then he got to the point.

"We've got a problem with Arnold Fulton's case," said the judge.

"What do you mean? This report proves he's guilty. It's the missing evidence!"

"The problem is he's already been found not guilty."

"No, *you* found him not guilty. The jury found him guilty."

"Under the law I didn't have any choice."

"Well, we've got rock solid evidence now. Let's just try him again."

"We can't try him again."

"Why not?"

"It would be unconstitutional under what we call double jeopardy."

"What the hell are you talking about? We've got absolutely solid proof that he was involved in crushing that little girl's hand!"

"We can't try him again for that, and we can't try the sheriff for obstruction of justice because they're not going to rat on each other. If Arnold reveals what happened with the report and the farm, he could be tried and convicted of obstruction of justice, so he's not going to tell anybody anything."

Burt sat there angry, incredulous.

"Are you telling me there's nothing the law can do to give that little girl justice?"

"That's what I'm telling you."

Burt sat there and stared at the judge. Then, without speaking, Burt stood up, put on his hat, and walked out of the house. The judge sighed and looked out the window and watched Burt drive away.

———◆———

Burt didn't press the issue with the sheriff, and he didn't tell the sheriff that he knew about the Swenson farm. He was sure the sheriff had forgotten about the envelope, and he was just as sure that the sheriff had never intended to give it to him. The sheriff had made a classic mistake. Once he had put the envelope in his desk drawer it was out of sight and thus out of mind, and he had failed to remove it from his desk and secrete it before somebody found it.

# THE MOOD

This time of year was ordinarily a cheerful time, a season of color and of harvest and of laying by in store for the year ahead. It was the beginning of the yearly pilgrimage of the outsiders to the mountain to feast on the color and other products of the mountain, and of course to leave some of their money with the mountain people.

It was amazing. The mountain people could go into the woods in the summer and cut down saplings and trim them to a length of about five feet and let them dry and then varnish them and call them walking sticks, and the outsiders would drive from a hundred miles away to pay good money for them.

This year the people still welcomed the money but there was no cheer in the air. The sun shone, and the autumn color appeared as it did every year, but a grey gloom hung over the people of the mountain and to them the colors were dulled and the air was heavy. People were still disgusted at the judge – or at least at the law. All over the mountain there was a pervasive sense of injustice, a notion that the law had failed them, that the law, which is supposed to be right, was in fact wrong. After the newspaper had published the judge's explanation of why he was required by the law to acquit Arnold Fulton even though the jury had voted for a conviction, and after the preachers had preached and cajoled and pled for peace on the mountain, and after they had discoursed and taught lessons on constitutional law and its application to this case, and after they had danced and leaped and gestured and pled some more, the people seemed to accept the explanation, but they didn't like it and they were mad and it bore heavily on them. It was pretty clear that there was a fatal gap in the evidence, and accepting the fact that a conviction must be based on the evidence, the people could understand why the judge had to do what he did. They accepted that there was a gap in the evidence, that there was something missing that prevented the law from finding Arnold Fulton guilty. But then when Burt Reedus found the missing shift report and sent it to the judge and it became public knowledge that the cars in front of Arnold Fulton's house were indeed the same cars as those in front of Tammy Allison's house the night of the attack, there was a public uproar, and everybody demanded that Arnold be tried again because the proof was now there. The man was guilty and everybody knew it. He needed to be punished! This in turn required a new explanation by the judge and the prosecutor and more preaching by the preachers that the Double Jeopardy Clause of the United States Constitution would not allow the people to try Arnold again even though the missing evidence had been discovered. The fact that the state could now prove that the two cars that were parked in front of the Fulton home were the same as those parked in front of the Allison home would still not permit a violation of the double jeopardy provision of the constitution. The law was clear and well settled.

The judge and the prosecutor both wrote letters to the editor of the newspaper explaining the Double Jeopardy Clause, but the people could not accept this. For the first time ever the races on the mountain were united in seeking justice against a white person who evidently had committed a grievous wrong against a Negro. And now the same system of law that they wished to apply in their pursuit of justice was going to prevent them from even beginning their pursuit within that system. It was hardly surprising that the Negroes and the Cherokee felt this way, but many were surprised that the white community was as frustrated as the rest for not being able to go after Arnold Fulton and put him away for awhile. It had become crystal clear to everyone that Arnold was guilty of crushing the hand of a little Negro girl who had become a musical phenomenon. He had deliberately and meanly taken this gift away from her forever, and there was in these people a goodness that was stronger than their history and that transcended race and that made them for a time despise their law. All the people except the Klan types were united in their disgust and frustration, and people gathered in little knots and talked of killing Dr. Arnold Fulton. They gathered in town, in Free Town, on Cherokee Ridge, and in the country stores scattered around the mountain.

"To hell with the law!" they would say. "It ain't right. Somebody needs to do something about this." But the judge kept telling the preachers that the law prohibited retrying Arnold and the preachers tried to explain this to their people, and things just got worse by the day. The preachers had lost the spirit; they could no longer leap and shout and gesture forcefully when they faced their people in the churches and other meeting places. They taught the people what the law was and the people listened, but they did not accept. And then here and there it started resurfacing. Somebody said if Arnold had been a Negro they would have found a way to retry him. That spread around the mountain and even some of the whites began to say that might be true. In their souls they *knew* it was true. Soon the younger black men started talking about using some of the guns the preachers had distributed last year, but they didn't know who they would shoot. The whites were on their side this time. The whole mountain got madder.

Back in town from his week of fishing and drinking the sheriff holed up in his office and watched the developments. He was getting a bit nervous about his dealings with Arnold coming to light, but as far as he knew, no one knew about the connection between Arnold and him. Everybody seemed to believe his story about finding the carbon copy of the shift report behind a file cabinet and putting it in his desk drawer. They even believed his story about Burt Reedus's name written in his handwriting on the envelope that had the report in it and that was found in his desk. When Burt confronted him about it he told Burt he had found it behind the file cabinet some time after the trial and that he had put the report in the envelope and had written Burt's name on it and stuck it in his desk drawer intending to give it to Burt the next evening, and then just forgot about it.

The sheriff was confident that Arnold would keep their secret because although Arnold could not be retried for the attack on Tammy Allison, he could be tried for obstruction of justice for destroying evidence, and would surely be convicted and would get the book thrown at him at sentencing. But they would both be safe as long as there was no evidence of their collusion.

No, Arnold will keep his mouth shut, because he's smart enough to know what they'll do to'im if he talks, and if we both lay low this will blow over after awhile. The major problem now is that the mountain's about to explode. The niggers are gettin' mean and the Cherokee are too quiet. They're planning something, maybe even with the niggers, and the niggers've got them guns now. God Almighty this could get messy!

He constantly revisited the Swenson farm deal, looking for any loose ends. Arnold had deeded the place to him outright, and he had registered the deed at the courthouse. He had signed a note for the purchase of the farm, just in case he had to answer how it was that he had the money from a sheriff's salary to pay for a farm as big as the Swenson farm, and he had an unregistered receipt signed by Arnold showing that the note had been paid in full. As far as he could tell there were no loose ends, but he worried about his circumstances all the time. Something just wasn't right. He knew these people and he knew that trouble lay ahead. He wished he could pull another five-day drunk right now.

# THE BOX

For three days after the judge met with Burt he was miserable. He looked in every legal corner he could imagine to find a solution to his problem. He had reviewed every possible legal approach to the problem, had read all the double jeopardy case law he could get his hands on, had called two judges that he respected and sought their insights into the double jeopardy issue. He canceled his appointments and rescheduled the few hearings that he had scheduled for that week. He went home and worked in his vegetable garden and messed with his pigs. He went back to his office and read and drank coffee and thought. He needed to talk to some people here who had a real sense of the mood of the mountain and would talk straight with him. The third day he called in his secretary and handed her a list.

"I want you to call these people and see if they can come by this afternoon around two o'clock and talk for a few minutes. Burt should be up by then."

———◆———

Shortly after 2 p.m. the judge sat in his office with Johnny Wolf, Minnie Fletcher, Charlie Caswell, and Burt Reedus. His secretary brought in cups and a pot of coffee. He reviewed the legal issues with them and got straight to the point.

"I'm at a dead end. I've done everything I can to figure out a way to get this thing back in court. I've even talked with two other judges about it but there's nothing there –

zero. The way I read the mood here on the mountain is that we've got trouble, but y'all are more in touch with the people than I am so I want to get your take on it. Got any ideas Johnny?"

"Judge, I've been goin' to church over in Free Town for the last three weeks, and I can tell you it's bad. I've never seen anything like it. The preachers are trying to do their job, but their folks are just sittin' there listenin' without nodding their heads or making a sound. As you well know that's not the way it's done in colored churches." The judge nodded. He was familiar with the way the colored preachers conducted their services. He visited different colored churches four or five times a year.

"What do you think Minnie?" She and the judge had gone to school together from the first grade through high school graduation. They didn't spend a lot of time together now but they were old friends.

"If you want to know what I really think, I think somebody's gettin' ready to get killed. This thing's a disaster! And the sorry part of it is, everybody on the mountain wants this man prosecuted, even the white folks – you know Jon, we've all got some good in us, all of us – but since we cain't prosecute'im it's got the colored people and the Cherokee mad at the whites, and I mean mad – fightin' mad, hurtin' mad! And you know why?"

"Why Minnie?"

"It's 'cause they see it as a white man's law that's lettin' him off, and I think they might be right about that. What do you think would happen here if a little twelve year old white girl had got her hand crushed by some colored men to keep her from bein' able to play the piano? To keep her from playin' in a competition that she had earned the right to enter by playing the best music that's ever been heard on this mountain? Answer me that."

He looked her in the eyes. What could he say?

She hadn't finished. "I guarantee ya there'd be justice somehow or another. It might not be your kinda so-called law, that stuff you dish out sittin' up there on the bench in that black robe, but there'd be some law applied from somewhere, and you know that as well as I do. And that's the way the people are feelin' – even the white people. But the white folks are scared 'cause they know it's a white man's law you're dishin' out and they know the coloreds and the Cherokee're gettin' bad mad about that. You let a man reach the point where he doesn't care if he dies and you got trouble, and I'm tellin' ya some of'em have reached that point – they're not scared to die. They're fed up with it and there's gonna be innocent blood all over the place before this is over!" She stopped and looked him straight in the face.

*Well spoken. There's no truth like that which comes out of a southern woman's mouth when she speaks her piece. Minnie's got it right. Hasn't it been a maxim in the law all the way back to old England that for every wrong there is a remedy? Where's the remedy here? Where is it?*

"Charlie?"

"Well, I'll tell ya, when I walk around over in Free Town, they're treatin' me differently than they used to. They don't talk to me much any more. They look at me and then look away or walk off and get busy doin' somethin.' And I've been seein' a lot more guns propped up beside people sittin' on their front porches in the last couple of weeks. It's not lookin' good. I think Minnie's tellin' it like it is. What you have to understand is that there's gonna be a solution to the problem – no question about it. Somebody's gonna fix this problem and no matter who does it, it's not gonna be peaceful. The way I see it is the people are holding back a little while to see if somebody takes care of the problem without the whole mountain having to raise up a ruckus with a bunch of people gettin' hurt or killed."

Everybody nodded.

"What're you seeing Burt? You drive around in Free Town just about every night, right?"

"I'm seein' the young men – and some of the older ones too – standin' around fires out in the yards a lot more than they normally do, and just about every night I see some of 'em holdin' rifles. And there's more yellin' and they're not laughin' any. And I'm seein' a lot more of the Cherokee men hangin' around Free Town than I've ever seen before. I mean a lot more! Somethin's getting ready to blow."

They left and the judge sat alone. It was cleaning day and the judge could hear Adsila, the little Cherokee woman that had married the ex-deputy, sweeping in his conference room next to his office. She tapped on the door that connected the two rooms and after a moment she stepped into the judge's office with her broom and cleaning supplies.

"Afternoon Judge. Should I come back later?"

"No, this is fine. I've just been sitting here thinking some."

She began dusting the flat surfaces in the room.

"Judge?"

"Yes Adsila?"

"Some of my people want me to ask you somethin' private."

"What's that Adsila?"

"They want me to ask you ain't they nothin' you can do?"

"What do they mean Adsila?"

"Judge, my people love you."

He was stunned. He looked at her and then had to look down quickly. He choked up for a moment. He couldn't handle much of this in his current condition.

She knew.

"Some of 'em says that if they's anybody on the mountain that can keep a lot of good folks from gittin' hurt, it's you. They don't want people to git hurt. They respect you and they love you Judge."

He swallowed and waited a long moment. *Lord Jesus help me get through this without breaking down in front of this little cleaning woman. I can't handle this.*

"Adsila, I've got to go home now and work with my pigs a little. When you finish up here you go back and tell your people to give me a little more time, and tell them I respect them too and I ... " He couldn't finish it. He jumped up and hurried out without saying anything more. Adsila began sweeping.

———◆———

Some things you just know. You don't know how you know it – you just know it. Sometimes you can step outside the situation and analyze everything that can be said about the thing that you know, and discover the reasons that you know the thing; but then you must ask yourself how you know that the reason is sufficient for knowing the thing. And it never ends. So you settle the matter yourself and move on. At some point you stop asking yourself the question and you move on. Or do you really stop asking the question? Maybe it's that constant question sitting there after each answer that makes you you. But to survive you stop asking the question – at least for a time – and you move on. There is a metaphysics. You move on and do what you have to do, no matter what the law says. You know it's right: We hold these truths to be self-evident: The organism must survive. Minnie Fletcher knows. Minnie Fletcher knows. Adsila knows. Adsila knows.

———◆———

In moments like these he turned to his poetry, for there he found direction, answers that dwelt in the scrivenings that he had set down over the years.

*Homo scribat!* Man writes! Like no other creature, man writes, and his writings reach out and engage and capture something. They are about something, and it is by returning to them that homo alone meets himself, again and again. Homo writes, and then revisits his words and lives and grows and re-encounters.

As he had many times before, the judge went to his study and took a sheaf of worn papers from his desk drawer.

He walked across the back yard to the pigpen and sat on a small bench next to the barn inside the enclosure. Three pigs waddled toward him from the far corner of the pen. He began to read.

# BOOK TWO
## HOMO

# CRISTOLOGO

A train whose name was Yesterday
Came thundering down that track.
You know the one.
That same track on which Tomorrow
    thundered in....
From east and west
A hundred thousand tons of steel
Came screaming,
Screaming down that track,
And crashed....

The track is gone,
The steel is gone,
The thing is done.
But if you will come along with me,
I will show you where it happened:
I was there,
Sitting on a bench,
In a little station,
In a village whose name was
    Now,
Waiting to catch my train.

So come with me, but know that you do not
    come this way
If not wonderingly, and open, and true;
This seeks discoverously;
This bespeaks, and apprehends and
    distributes ambiguously;
(Are you listening?)
This weeps and laughs and hurts.
This points to certain secrets that will
    delight you.

# PROLEGOMENA

## TO ANY FUTURE METAPHYSICS

Deus.
Homo.
Homodeus.
Deus.

# PART ONE

## HILDA

### I

The old man raised his hand and slashed it down hard. It met neck right behind the creature's ears. There was a solid crunch and a brief convulsion.

The old man immediately took a sharp steel blade and cut the creature's head off and then let the carcass hang there and bleed. This must be done before the heart stopped pumping. Then he cut the skin around each hind leg, cut across the crotch, severed the front feet, and peeled the hide down. He drew the guts, then cut the organ meat from them to keep for himself, and tossed the rest to his dogs. He broke the hind legs at the first joint and cut through them there with his blade, and then he tossed the carcass into a wooden box that earlier he had half filled with snow. He filled the box with more snow, covering the creature; the meat would be more easily cut after it chilled. He picked up the box and walked into his cabin.

## 2

The night had come, and the old man now walked in the forest. Snow flew about his boots as they ploughed deep, marking a trail to tell the occasional wanderer whence he had come.

But the wanderer in this forest, for the moment, was he.

The old house deep therein had been good for him; he eventually found himself there when he was tired and needed to ponder. There, in the night, he could be rested.

He raked the snow from a spot on the porch and sat.

He watched – the distant winking windows; chimney sparks showering down on moonlit scapes...

High, high fly the yearning spirits;
High fly the seekers;
High fly the comers and the goers,
And the gazers at the comers and the goers,
And the gazers at these;
And the greeters and the talkers –
     Ah, the greeters and the talkers –
How high they fly...

At first the old man thought about her.
He pondered the thing.
He was at peace most of the time
But when he went deeper and deeper,
Remembering the blood, and the pain, and the tears
It was then that those recollections transformed him. He
    went deeper and deeper,
Till anguish tore at his gnawing, boiling innards;
He saw her and the dead baby
And afterwards he saw her dead,
While he waited and wondered,
And watched for the dawn...

I'll spend these deep, dark seasons
Where howling winds blow cold and fierce,
And roaring flames rage hot, and long,
And where searing memories of you, my Love,
Sustain me through the long, long night.

Breathe into me, holy Lord of all,
And be my muse,
That from this come truth alone,
And that when these words
Have failed to exhibit the fullness of
Your immense, immeasurable holiness,
As they shall,
I will somehow bow me further down,
And let you take me home.

Then slowly out of the night they came. Slowly, out of
the bedded leaves,
from deep in the caves,
stretching and gazing about they came,
moving away from the dens,
and the night,
and the night mind,
and out onto the pebbly slopes,
leading down below,
where the dew-tender grains of the wild-grass patch awaited
    them.

I've looked out across you,
And seen the whole of you,
And seen your comings and your goings,
Homo;
And I've seen you recline as one across whole lands,
And I've seen you rise all with the dawn,
And take up your tools and your weapons,
And set out upon your roads and your byways,
And into the forests,
And assert yourself.

And your groupings of habitations have amazed me,
Homo.

Domus!
Civitatem! How can I speak of them?
How can I tell of the application of your paws
To the earth and the stone and the wood,
And the mixing of your mortar,
And the shaping of your spikes,
And then with them the making of your hut,
And then the placing of another and another
Till there are many, together;
You congregate, Homo!

I have long sought to view you from a metaspecial perspective,
And yet I cannot do it;
I cannot do it completely, Homo,
For your utterances make sense to me,
And your motions are my motions:
There have been times when I would have
Locked my paw around a club,
And a stout one, too!
And set out meanly upon the trail
Toward yon agglomeration
To injure and to kill:
I know you Homo.

## (THE RESOLUTION)

*The hunter crouched in the glade, in the tall grass,*
*And slowly, silently, took one long arrow from his pouch*
*And nocked it; he must not let this moment pass*
*Without its long awaited, long sought resolution.*

*The hunted paused, in the shade, by the tall grass,*
*And rested, kneeling, full aware that his ablution,*
*In the temple, had resolved nothing alas,*
*For the one who would have his soul, who crouched in the*
*    glade.*

*The hunter aimed his arrow, from the tall grass,*
*And drew it; and every fiber in him tensed, replayed*
*The passions of a thousand pains that would never pass,*
*And then released. Watching, the hunter slowly rose from his*
*    crouch.*


And the poet was the one who watched the ones who
watched the ones who gathered grain in the wild-grass
patch.

## 3

I am the storyteller's poet,
Admirer of threads and of
    threads of threads,
And willing talker thereabout.
I seek all their connections.

I am that percipient essence before which
    there is the ceaseless query.
Perhaps it could even be said of me
    that I am the query.
(It is true that from time to time
I succumb to the machinations of man;
But in the end I am true to you,
My Song,
For in the end it is the poet who sings.)

# 4

From among those beings in the dim past
he had wandered, and had gone on.

Why? He had asked, and had gone on, till
he came to the brink of the deep, and looked.

It is too late, he said.

And the chasm returned with the reply,
Why?

He died! He cried.

Said the chasm, Who?

Me!

You?

Yes, he muttered, and gazed,

From the brink of the deep,

To the opposite shore.

Said the chasm, Where?

There, he said, and pointed from the
brink to the opposite shore.

Then why are you here?

Here?

I don't know, he said, and gazed,
from the brink of the deep,
to the opposite shore.

## 5

The baby's half dead
And I'm about to freeze.

Put some wood on that fire!

Mama's sick and cain't work no more.

What d'yuh mean there ain't none?
Go chop some.
I'm cold.

I'm sick and tired o' the whole rotten,
        stinkin' mess,
You hear me?

These sheets stink.
Seems yuh could at least get some more sheets.

Then wash 'em! They stink.
And quit lookin' at me that way.
It's not my fault they busted up m' still.

Ed was gonna fix the leak on the roof
        this mornin'
But the damn law took his scooter,
And the shingles were in the saddlebag.
The stupid idiot ought to have carried 'em
        in his hand dammit,
I don't care if it is cold.

All for two measly pints o' licker,
And I betcha they drank a pint o' licker
And claimed there wont but one pint
I'll guaran damn tee it.

Sam,
Go get them burlap sacks,
And nail'em down on the roof.

Don't you argue with me, boy,
Or I'll kick your teeth in,
You hear me?
Now get up there.

Damn roof.
It's cold as sin
And I can't even keep dry.

Put some WOOD on that fire!

Hilda, I'm goin' to the store.

## II

Damn rain.

# III

Hey Jim.
Gimme some matches.

Cold, ain't it?

Where's Bud,
After that fancy stuff up the road?

You reckon he'll get it?

I'm gonna tell yuh somethin',
Yuh never can tell.
They say her old man's got money.
I'd like to get my hands on it.

Well, be seein' yuh.

# IV

House oughta be warm by now... .

# V

Hilda?

HILDA!

You answer me woman, when I call you,
You hear me?

Now shut that baby up.
I'm sick and tired o' hearin' that
    fuss ever' minute I'm home.
There ain't no peace o' mind around here.

What d'yuh mean she's hungry?
Feed'er yuh idiot.

What d'yuh mean there ain't no milk?
I bought'er a can day before yesterday!

Shut up,
I ain't got no money.
And quit cryin', will yuh?
Yuh make me nervous....

Hilda, come'ere.

Take this cigar back to the store
And tell'em to give yuh a can o' milk.

I just bought it a little while ago,
And it ain't broke,
So they oughta trade it.
AND SHUT UP THAT CRYIN', WILL YUH!

Take my coat.
And don't you break that cigar,
You hear me woman?
Now go on.

Stupid baby oughta eat fatback,
Like me and the rest.

Ma, you feelin' okay?

Git'er another quilt Liz.

Huh?

Then give'er mine and shut up.

WAIT A MINUTE, don't.
Ma, I'll put my coat over yuh when
      Hilda gets back.
It'll dry out.
Put some WOOD on that damn fire!

Damn, that woman better not break my cigar.

Oh Lord, I forgot to tell'er about the HOLE!
That stupid woman,
If that cigar fell out it'll get soaked,
And even if I find it they won't take
      it back,

And she won't get no milk,
And the baby'll scream all night!

I"m goin' after Hilda.
Y'all keep that baby warm,
You hear me?

## VI

Damn rain.

Maybe she didn't put it in the pocket.
Maybe....

Huh? Is that her comin' yonder? Hilda?

HILDA! Yuh didn't drop my cigar?

It wont broke?

Cold ain't it? Gimme my coat.

Naw, keep the filthy thing.
And shut up that cryin'.

Aw come'ere Hilda.
Don't cry.
We'll be home in a minute.

# VII

PUT SOME WOOD ON THAT DAMN FIRE!
It's cold in here, I'm tellin' yuh.
And give that baby some milk.

The roof ain't leakin' no more, Hilda.
I told yuh them burlap sacks'ud do it.
You okay Ma?
Think I'll go to bed....
Come'ere Hilda.

# 6

My mare I mount, and she gathers.
She gathers and she holds.
(No tears my lady – who can at once
        weep and sing?)
She gathers, till we can no more.
She holds, till we can no more.

Princess?

And then together
We fly!

# 7

We know not why the roles of yesterday
    were played,
Nor why tomorrow's greatest dreams
    are never lived.
We know not yet why blood was spilled
    and children cried,
(All the children God has made
    have cried)
Nor why tomorrow blood and tears
    will flow again.
But this we know:
Now this we know:
In a little room, in a little house,
    we make love today.

## NOSOTROS

I've gone into you, Woman of earth,
Screaming my way into your soul
    in that primal moment.
Your rhythms mine, and mine yours,
We've found the path,
And journeyed it together.

In that place where pangs of fear
    seize the soul of man,
Where cries of self-sorrow
    and the gnawing
    and the gnashing
Sound out loudly from this infernal tumult,
I center,
And move on.

Sound the cadence!
Stomp, Stomp,
Here or there a pleasure,
On beyond a woe.

Stomp, Stomp,
On down through the halls of time
We make our way.

One cold day, beneath snow-laden pines,
the old man made his way toward the village.
He had come out of his cabin in the tiny clearing
and had found his path and walked for
awhile; now he came out of the forest and stopped,
and looked toward the village.

He was not too cold; he had long been a man
in the forest, so it was tolerable.

On this day there was no wind. There was
silence – snow silence. The old man stood there
for a moment and looked, and then he set out
across the fields toward the village.

# 9

And the old man looked across the fields
and the hills and the forests, and he thought:

Utterly yours I am,
You have given me joy
And bathed me in sorrow;
You have made me see
And left me blind -
And still, I am awed.
Still, I am awed.

ECSTASY!
World within or wherever you may be,
We know you not
For you retreat,
And we know not where.
We know not why, nor how,
But we must assume you have your reasons,
Else you would take our hands,
And walk us through those realms
    we call ecstasy.

Do you know that you torture me?
Do you know that you let me stare
And that you cause me to wonder
And that you tantalize me?
And yet you keep your secret.
Do you know that you beckon me,
        and then retreat?

A night wanderer you have caused me to be,
A star gazer uncertain,
Till you settle about me
And speak truth to me.

Engage me!
Do not hesitate to trust me with your
        cherished knowledge.
Teach me your secrets -
I'll harbor them and use them,
        and I'll pass them on to those,
And those only,
Who should have them.

My mane is white.
Today it falls about my shoulders,
   flowing.
Tomorrow it may be blowing in the wind.
That I know,
For I have learned.

   And then the old man stepped out of the
field and onto the road leading into the village.

## 10

The people who were gathered had asked him to come out of his little cabin deep in the forest and into the village, for a great question was to come before them on the morrow.

From among those gathered there in the village that day, there first arose three wise men. And they all said in unison,
   The universe is our home.
And then the first wise man said,
   Be it ever so humble.
And then the second wise man said,
   Be it ever how you wish.
And then the third wise man said,
   It is.
And then the three wise men sat down.

## II

Then the old man rose and looked at the
people, and the people looked at him.

And a child of the village said to the
old man,

Would you tell us a story?

And the old man was filled with joy, and
he looked at the child, and he loved it. He had been here
many times before, and had told them many stories.
He knew the child within was saying, Where are
you going? Can I go with you?

And the old man said,

Yes, my little friend, I will tell you
the story of a lamb. Listen...listen.

## 12

# THE LAMB

In a village in another land, a little boy walked down the
street beside a baby elephant. The elephant belonged to the
boy's family, and it was the boy's job to feed and water the
elephant each day. In that land elephants were very important to the people, for they were used to lift and move
things that were too heavy for the people to lift; and when
the people of the village had to journey long distances, they
rode their elephant if it was their good fortune to have one.
The task of caring for a baby elephant was a very important
task indeed for a little boy, because the little elephant would
grow up someday, and then he would spend the rest of his
life helping the people of the village. The little boy was
proud that his family had enough faith in him to let him care
for their baby elephant.

The sun was shining brightly at this time of day and almost everyone in the village had gone inside his house to
escape the heat. The boy walked the little elephant to a water trough which was right at the edge of the village. The
elephant began to drink and to spray water over his body
with his trunk. The cool water felt good.

The little boy decided to lie down in a shaded spot not
far from the trough to get out of the hot sunshine. He lay
down on the cool ground and watched his family's baby elephant drink and play in the water.

Lying there on the ground in the shade relaxed the little
boy so much that pretty soon it was easier for him to keep
his eyes closed than it was to keep them open. Very soon he
was sound asleep.

The baby elephant played in the water for awhile and

then drank some more, till he had had enough. After awhile he was ready to go back, or do something else.

He walked over to the little boy and gently touched him with the end of his trunk, but the boy was so soundly sleeping that this failed to wake him. The elephant stood there for a few minutes and then touched the boy again, but he kept on sleeping. So the baby elephant decided that he would do something else while his little friend slept.

For some time now, when he would come to drink and play at the water trough, the little elephant had looked at the fields around the village and at the woods beyond the fields. He had often thought it would be nice to walk through the fields and to go into the woods and play for awhile. Today he decided that since he couldn't wake his little friend, he would take that walk that he had been thinking about.

The little elephant ambled through the fields in soft dirt that felt really good to his feet, but what he wanted to do more than anything else was to go into the woods, so he walked on toward them.

Soon the little elephant came to the edge of the woods, and looked in. It was so pretty and cool-looking in there. Everything looked soft and clean and mellow. He decided to walk right on in and explore some.

The woods smelled good. And the baby elephant discovered that when he rubbed against the rough bark of a tree, it felt good. After he had scratched himself for awhile, he walked on, going deeper into the woods. He would see something interesting over this way and he would come have a look at it. Then he would see something else over that way and he would go have a look at that. He rambled all around and did this for a while and really had a lot of fun.

But it wasn't long before he began to get tired. So he decided it was about time to go on back home. The baby elephant started back the way he thought he should, but the more he walked the stranger the trees and bushes looked to him. But he really wanted to go home, so he kept on walking.

Finally the little elephant came to a small clearing and in

the middle of it was a pool that was about knee-deep to him. He decided that he would wade into the pool and rest himself there for a few minutes, for by now he was getting really tired of walking and he knew how good the cool water would feel to his feet. He waded in and drank some, and then sprayed his back with water. It felt really good. But after a few more minutes of this, the baby elephant decided it was time to start walking again.

Just as he was getting ready to come out of the pool, he heard a rustling noise a good distance away.

Since elephants are big even when they are babies, the baby elephant couldn't hide behind a tree or bush. He just stood there and looked in the direction of the noise. He could hear it getting closer and closer, but he just kept standing there in the pool in the little clearing, looking. And then, right out of the bushes and right into the clearing trotted a baby lion.

Big lions can hurt baby elephants, but when they are still young, lions and elephants are not afraid of each other. They just think about things like playing together. And that is just what the baby elephant started thinking about. He raised his trunk and made a happy sound through his mouth and started splashing over toward the baby lion to smell him and play some. But the little lion wouldn't pay any attention to him. He just trotted right through the clearing with his nose close to the ground.

The elephant still wanted to play, though, so he ambled along behind the baby lion, trying to get his attention, but the lion just kept on trotting, with his nose close to the ground, and with the little elephant ambling along behind him.

Soon they were deep into the woods again, and they just kept on going. The baby elephant had his attention focused on his little lion friend and completely forgot about trying to find his way home.

Pretty soon the baby lion, with the baby elephant right behind him, came to the edge of the woods and stepped into a field. He didn't even slow down. He just kept his nose to the ground and trotted on and the baby elephant stayed right behind him because he still wanted to play some as soon as the little lion got to wherever he was going.

The baby lion kept trotting and the elephant kept ambling along behind him. And then, all of a sudden, the little elephant looked up and what he saw made him feel good all over. He was home. He was right at the edge of the little village where he lived.

The baby lion stopped and sniffed around for a moment, and then trotted off in another direction, with his nose still close to the ground. He never did pay any attention to the little elephant who wanted to play with him. The elephant watched him go across the field toward some other woods, and pretty soon he disappeared.

The sun was almost down now, and the little elephant wanted to drink some more water and then get back to his family. He walked around the edge of the village till he came to the water trough. There was the little boy, still asleep. The baby elephant drank some water and then walked over to wake the little boy. He touched him with his trunk and the boy jumped up and said, Oh, No! The sun is about to set! We've got to go right home!

That night, at supper, the father said to his family, Tomorrow we hunt the old lion. She came today and took a lamb.

# 13

The old man looked at the child for a long moment, and said no more. Then he looked long at the people, saying nothing, and then he turned and left the village, and went back across the fields and back onto the trails leading back to the tiny cabin deep within the forest.

And then that night the old man left his cabin and once again found himself a moonlit path.

They ask me what is truth!
Here is truth:
I've gone down the dark road lost,
Then found my way and blissed in light.
And then,
My friends,
I tell you,
In spite of all in me,
I've turned,
And gone back down that dark road lost.

Here is truth:
The rose and the serpent slept together.
The dawn came
And the rose bloomed and spread;
From dewdrops on fragrant petals
Light burst forth,
And we saw life.
Then came the cold,
And into the deepest folds of darkness
The serpent slithered.
Into his abode he drew us,
And it was dark and dismal.
The breath of fear and pain and hate
        touched us,
And we saw death.

They ask me what is truth?
They give me the morrow's question
    this day?
What is truth?
Here is truth:
That of all that is,
That speaks from every dimension
    of every essence,
That singularly undeniable statement,
Made by the rock and made by the bird,
Made by the sun and made by the wind,
And by the stars, and by the tears
    and by the pain,
And by the joys and by the hate,
And the sounds and the universes,
And the songs, the screams, the explosions,
    and the implosions,
And the crashes,
Here and in all spaces,
And beyond them –
That about all this,
ALL,
That simply says, I am –
That, he thought, is truth.

# 14

That night clear white light shone in the moonlit forest. Clear white light that bathed the paths and trails that led to the fields and roads and villages, and to a tiny cabin in a tiny clearing.

But that night the paths and the trails to the tiny cabin in the tiny clearing were no more trod.

They found the old man some time later. In the evening they laid him out on a slab of stone in the forest.

Soon he was gone.

Gone?

## 15

When all is done,
When day is gone
And dusk has faded;
And when I know that I have heard my song,
And looked upon it and considered it,
    and smiled,
Then, I turn gently toward
    the fatherland.

Then I must go my way,
For this is the way the world is.
Likewise, you must go yours.
I cannot be with you when you come upon
    your first hurdle,
Nor can I open those doors you closed,
For this is the way the world is.
I cannot comfort you nor can I brush
    tears from your cheeks
When you weep for something you know not.
For now, I must be without you,
For this is the way the world is.
We must walk away,
And walk, and walk, and walk,
Till our paths shall converge,
And we shall move hand in hand
Through a world we've come to know.

# 16

As you go yonder way,
Mark a path there for me.
I'm going that way too,
When I finish here.

## 17

Gone, my Love, are the high winds and the
     soaring eagles.
Grim is the night.
Dim are the night beings and the night mind;
Gone is the light.

# PART TWO

## HAWKNESS

### I

I come.
I present myself.
I make my statement:
The songs I shall sing to you,
    peoples of the universe,
Will be of my essence;
It can be no other way,
And you must know that now.

I accept the call, but I come to you
    poet.
The man is gone.
The causes, the theories, the isms,
    the differences, the what-ifs,
The great and the small,
    yesterday and tomorrow,
Gone.
Just feeling being now,
My joys and my sorrow concurrent
    on one blissful hum,
The hum of the harmony of all the
    systems of it all,
The hum of God,
The path.

Be it now known to all that
    henceforth the doctorates,
    the misterates, the madamates,
    the sirs, the honorables,
    the dishonorables,
Force me no more.
For you I am the poet,
Nothing more, nothing less.
And for me, you are the poet,
nothing more, nothing less.

**2**

I engage your eyes,
And I see that you know.
And you, you know that I know, and so,
Our brotherhood undeniable,
Peace flows between us and becomes us,
And we are one.

How high we soar!
To you, my love, I lay these presents down.
To you all I have and shall have forever.
Awed I am, and shall be forever.
To you my song I sing.

High, so high we soar!
And I see the nations
        of man the animal,
And I see delineations,
And I tell you each and every one
they will fade away.

I come to you with power
        incomprehensible,
For I have dreamed,
And I have perceived the family
        of sapiens.
We soar...

## 3

On this day I am the hawk.
I dive,
And all the hawks of all
    the ages,
Before and to come,
Rush on this dive.

(For one brief moment,
In the totality of it all,
This form is here,
In the all-being.
It blinks into shape once,
It quivers,
And then it is gone.
Gone.
But something goes on.

It's there in the storyteller's soul,
And in the marble cornerstone
    of homo's domicile,
This thing that moves on
    through us all,
And does not stop when
    each we do,
But moves on,
Becoming more with
    each birth,

And yet even more with
    each demise,
Transversing generations and
    constituting them each,
Expressing them all,
And being expressed by them,
This thing.

So this song issues from it all.
As much yours as mine it is,
and no claim to it shall be held
    lest it be in favor of all.)

Imagine!
The whole thing, at once
    shuddering, trembling, rumbling,
As earthward we rush on this dive,
Anticipators of the scream of contact,
Of this moment's truth:
The union the Word:
A morsel in our gut,
That all the children of all our children
    of all the ages,
May dive.

# 4

God All.
God the tree.
God the bird. God grass.
God fences and pastures.
God cows, horses, mules, and pigs.
God leaves, water, and stone.
God the highs, God the hassles, God
    the smooth sailing.
God the illusions of man,
    God you, God me,
God All.

# 5

Go into the night!
Count every star in the heavens.
Go roam the valleys,
And climb the mountains,
And sail the oceans:
Then come to me and let me gently
     whisper in your ear -
I'll say to you, In all time,
You will not see what I have perceived
     in one timeless flash.

# 6

I've stood at the foot of the mountain
　　and looked up.
I've soared to the peak
　　and looked down.
I've stood inside
　　and looked out,
I've stood outside
　　and looked in.

So come, my friends,
Sail to me on those gentle waters,
And see that I shall
　　enfold you,
And dwell with you and in you forever,
And shall never, ever leave you.
Now come.

# 7

But know you this: From my soul will I sing as much as
     from my mind.
If thinker you would have me
     always be,
You will go wanting,
For poet I am,
I am.

# BOOK THREE
# THE RESOLUTION

# LAW

Suddenly his mind snapped back to now and to the gilt that was rubbing against his leg, and he was back at the pigpen and he had made a decision. He scratched the little black hog and she wanted more.

The situation on the mountain had never been this grave. For decades he had administered justice here on this mountain; he had sworn his solemn oath of commitment to the law – to see that wrongs were remedied, that crimes were punished, that all people on this mountain stood equal before the law. And now there was a heinous wrong that had been committed, and all the people knew of this wrong, and there was no law within this system to which he had sworn his solemn oath that would remedy this evil. The people were demanding law, and there was no law to give them. But now he knew – he knew – what he had to do if this problem was to be fixed. He had always loved the law, but now he almost hated it. It had failed his people, and Minnie, that kid from forty years ago, now that woman who could talk the fire out of you, had given him what he needed: she had talked some fire *into* him.

There was some law for this, a higher law, and the people knew it and demanded it. He saw it – Adsila, the blossom, the plump sweet little Cherokee with her simple words, had helped him see it: The law was made for man, not man for the law. There would be no wrong in this, and a wrong would be made right. The spark inside him had turned to flame, and now it burned. These were his people, all of them. Minnie had helped him. Sweet, simple little Adsila had helped him.

———•———

"We're going on a little vacation today!" Mama yelled down the stairs to J.C. and me. It was early and J.C. and I were still in bed. I had heard Mama and Daddy traipsing around the house after we went to bed, and before I fell asleep I heard Daddy say he was going to call Luigi. This morning I had heard them moving around in the kitchen at least an hour before they yelled down to us. They had already eaten their breakfast and packed some suitcases and were taking stuff to the car.

"When?"

"As soon as you get washed up and eat your breakfast."

"What about school?"

"Don't worry about school."

"Why didn't y'all tell us about this before now?"

"We just decided last night after you went to bed. Daddy and I decided it's time to take a vacation. He wants to go see Luigi and Gabriella."

"Who's gonna feed the pigs and the chickens?"

"Daddy's already been over to Charlie's to see about getting him to come over and feed and check on the place every day till we get back. He called Luigi in Chicago last night and they said come on. So we're going! You want to come along?"

Luigi was one of Daddy's buddies from law school. It had been about two years since we had been to see him. I always enjoyed getting on the road and going somewhere, and once we got there it was awesome. On that earlier trip we stayed with Luigi and sweet Gabriella, and Mama and Daddy took us for walks along the shore of the lake, which looked like a sea to me. They had taken us to the Art Institute of Chicago, a huge art museum, where we spent an entire day looking at paintings and sculpture.

"Can we go to the art museum again?" J.C. asked sleepily. He loved art.

"You bet we can."

He really was an artist, even when he was young. At age 10 he could already draw a person so that I could tell who it was.

We left a half hour later and drove through mountains and valleys for several hours. Every couple of hours we stopped at a gas station or truck stop and Mama and Daddy would get a cup of coffee and we would all go to the bathroom, always to the ones marked Whites Only. We finally got out of the mountains down onto flatter country, which fascinated me. I was used to seeing mountains everywhere around me, and when I got to flat country I felt like I was really traveling, and I felt like I could see so much farther than back on the mountain. Later in life I learned to my surprise that people from flat country felt the same about being in the mountains. They felt that they could see much farther than they could down on flat country, and this exhilarated them.

We spent the night in Indianapolis. Daddy had been there a few times and he took us to a restaurant that he knew about. We ate well, and when we got back to the hotel Mama and Daddy let J.C. and me sit with them in the hotel bar and drink Cokes while they had drinks and watched the other people. I had never thought of Daddy to be much of a people watcher, but that night he appeared to be absorbed in viewing the crowd and the comings and the goings at the bar. We got up early the next morning, ate breakfast at the hotel, and headed out for Chicago.

We swung into Luigi's driveway late that afternoon and he and Gabriella were out the door and at our car before we came to a stop. There were happy hugs and kisses all around and exclamations about how much J.C. and I had grown since our last visit and grabbing suitcases and talking about supper and drinks before we even got to the front porch. Luigi talked about how pretty Mama was and Daddy talked about how pretty Gabriella was and we all jumped around and went inside to the smells of a Sicilian kitchen.

After supper – they called it dinner – Daddy took me and J.C. into Luigi's study and Mama and Gabriella went into the kitchen. The study was a big room lined with books. There were several stuffed leather chairs and we all took a seat. Luigi offered Daddy a cigar and to my surprise he accepted. Luigi extended the open cigar box to me and J.C. We were each in a chair sitting on our hands. We both smiled and shook our heads. Luigi smiled and opened a window and he and Daddy lit up and settled back to talk. Daddy asked Luigi how his practice was coming along and they talked about criminal defense work in Chicago and how that kept Luigi so busy that he didn't do any other kind of law now.

"Who would have ever thought twenty years ago that I would end up doing nothing but criminal defense work?" said Luigi.

"It's simple," Daddy said. "You were always the scholar, Luigi, and no other kind of practice gives you so many opportunities to confront the great constitutional issues. I simply cannot imagine you sitting in an office drafting deeds or corporate documents all day long. You're doing what you were made to do."

They sipped their drinks and smoked slowly. I was fascinated to see Daddy smoking the cigar because he almost never smoked, and J.C. just sat there taking it all in, obviously proud that he had been invited in with the men.

Luigi studied his glass and twisted it back and forth by the stem. "I guess you're right, but no one at Harvard ever suggested that we should go into criminal law. The big thing was corporate and securities law if you wanted a real career. Still is I guess."

"You're making a good living Luigi, and you're keeping the prosecutors on their toes. You're making them turn their corners at ninety degree angles instead of taking all those shortcuts they're prone to take."

Luigi looked at his cigar, flicked the one inch of ash into an ash tray, and sipped his drink.

"I *am* making a good living, but part of the price I have to pay is being looked down on by many for defending some of these high profile people in the so-called crime families."

Daddy nodded. "We both know that's just part of the business. The worst of them has a right to the best defense available and to a fair, constitutional trial."

"How about you, how's the judging going?"

Daddy told him about the happenings on our mountain, about the way our town was growing, about interesting cases that he had heard in the last couple of years, and then he started talking about Tammy Allison and what had happened to her. He started at the beginning and talked about the first competition and the way the audience reacted, and then he talked about the next night when Tammy placed first and Louise was runner-up and how that was the first time in her life that she had ever been a runner up. And then he talked about what happened to Tammy shortly after the competition.

Luigi listened.

Daddy told Luigi what a struggle it had been getting a prosecutor to move forward with the case, and how the supreme court had authorized him to appoint a special prosecutor. Daddy talked about Tammy's crushed hand and described what it looked like in the photographs that were introduced at the trial. He talked about the trial and the not guilty verdict that he had had to issue even though the jury had found Arnold Fulton guilty, and then he talked about deputy Burt Reedus and how he had found a report that had been missing and he talked about how the report showed that the license plate numbers in the report that Burt had seen at Dr. Fulton's home were the same as those that Charlie had seen in front of the Allison house. Then he talked about how he had gone down to the register of deeds office there in the courthouse and had seen that Arnold Fulton had deeded a farm to Sheriff Sam Bartlett shortly after Tammy's hand was crushed. Then for quite some time Daddy and Luigi talked about double jeopardy. Then Daddy talked extensively about the mood on the mountain and about how things were getting ready to explode.

Luigi puffed his cigar, took a sip of his brandy, and stared at Daddy. "So that's why you came."

"Yes," Daddy nodded.

"Okay. Let me pour you a little more brandy. Or come to think of it how about a little glass of grappa that Gabi and I brought back from Palermo last year? It's the best I've ever tasted." Luigi took out two fresh glasses and took a bottle from his liquor cabinet and poured the grappa. He handed Daddy a glass and then took his and held it up and they clinked glasses. I swear I could see his hand trembling.

"I'll ask around and see what I can find out Jon. How much time?"

"Two weeks max."

I looked at Daddy and saw something I had seen only once before, when our dog Lady died. He had tears in his eyes.

We stayed a couple more days, one of which was spent entirely at the Art Institute of Chicago. J.C. was happy, and I actually enjoyed myself too. For the remainder of our time in Chicago Daddy had me and J.C. with him every minute that he and Luigi were together. Then we headed back south.

# BACK FROM CHICAGO

Sometimes the gloom that visits the mountain does not derive from the weather. It comes from the people. It is a dark spirit that arises from their disgust, from their sense of hopelessness in the face of a raw, naked evil that has not been and apparently cannot be vindicated. Thus it was upon our return from Chicago; we came back into town to fair weather but the mood was dark and ugly and heavy. There were no smiles. Nobody would look anybody in the eye. The Negroes gathered after dark in bunches around little bonfires on vacant lots in Free Town. Some carried rifles or shotguns. The deputies kept their distance from them. The Cherokee parked their pickups in groups on Main Street and stood around mumbling to each other. They wouldn't look at any of the white people. The white people looked at the rifles and shotguns in the racks of the Cherokees' pickups as they drove into town. The deputies kept their distance from them too. The white people stayed home, tending their gardens and feeding their pigs and chickens and pulling grass for their rabbits, grumbling about the mood on the mountain.

The sheriff had holed up in his house and only occasionally stepped into Jack's for coffee. The atmosphere was glum there as well. Dr. Fulton went to the hospital when he had to, and stayed home otherwise. Blair Fulton kept her routine and stayed drunk. Oddly she was an early riser, often having breakfast by five-thirty in the morning. Breakfast consisted of eggs, toast, coffee, and bourbon. Her daytime entertainment consisted mostly of snarling at Arnold, planning what food should accompany her bourbon at lunch, watching

Louise mope and cry and kick the cats, and driving around town with Louise in the late afternoon and evening. She was inebriated by noon, but never appeared to be under the influence until she passed out at night. She had no trouble taking her daily drive, and the deputies left her alone as long as she stayed away from downtown. In this season of despair and gloom she was probably the least troubled person on the mountain.

———•———

The morning after he returned from Chicago the judge told his secretary to call the Negro preachers and see if they could meet with him that evening around seven o'clock. He sent her to the high school with a note for Johnny Wolf to come to the meeting. The group met in the judge's office at the courthouse.

The mood was somber; there were no pleasantries.

"I think this will blow over in about three weeks. Can you all keep the lid on for a while longer? I know you're doing your best but we've got to try to hold on just a little longer. I've got a feeling that somehow or another we're gonna see this thing worked out soon."

They looked at each other.

"What do you have in mind Judge?" one of them asked.

He didn't answer. He looked at them one by one. "Just tell me. Can we make it for another three weeks?"

After a moment Johnny Wolf said he could take care of that with the Cherokee. He didn't have any questions.

The preachers said they thought they could manage it, but it was going to take some stretching and some mighty hard preaching.

Everybody went home.

# AT ARNOLD'S PLACE
## AFTER CHICAGO

A little over a week after we got back from Chicago, traffic on the mountain increased dramatically. It was that time of year when the daily population on the mountain doubled or even tripled. People drove from hundreds of miles away to spend two or three days to wonder at the autumn colors of southern Appalachia. The downtown hotel stayed full through this season, and every roadside inn and rooming house on the mountain turned away travelers daily. Ordinarily this was a time of high spirits, for these visitors brought with them hard cash and left a decent amount of it in our fair town and scattered about our mountain. In return they took with them jellies and pumpkins and pickles and walking sticks and many other products that the people cheerfully sold to them at four times the normal local price.

It was the perfect time for the men to come in from New Jersey unnoticed. They parked their car down the street from the Fulton house and waited until the Negro servants and the woman and the girl left in separate vehicles. They had been watching the house for three days and had determined that this was an evening ritual. The target would come home at half past five and the servants and the woman and the girl would leave about half an hour later for an hour or so, mother and daughter in one vehicle and the servants in another.

This time, as soon as the servants and the woman and girl left, the men got out of their car, strolled the half block to the driveway, walked to the back door and entered. They were quick; they found Arnold in the kitchen. The handlers jumped him and drug him down the hall and forced him into a chair beside the table in his study. They closed the study door.

There were three of them, two handlers and the smaller man with the bow tie. The handlers secured Arnold to the chair with several wraps of duct tape around his torso, leaving his arms loose but tying them together at the wrists.

Bow Tie waited until Arnold was immobilized, then spoke.

"Sir, I don't know what you've done, but you have certainly incurred the wrath of some of our friends in Chicago."

"Chicago? I've never been to Chicago!"

"Apparently word of your deeds preceded you there."

"What are you talking about? What are you going to do? Please don't do this, please. I can give you money or land or whatever you want. I have plenty of both."

"Sir, it wouldn't be right for us to take money from you when we've already been paid for our services. We're not going to kill you."

"What are you going to do?" Arnold was losing his breath. He looked at the little man. The man had small delicate hands that could have been a surgeon's or a musician's hands.

"My instructions are to destroy most of the functioning of your hands. The man who sent us instructed me that when you are fully healed from what we do here today the only thing you should ever be able to do with your hands, either of them, is wipe yourself and feed yourself, and that with utmost difficulty. He said he doesn't even want you to be able to play with yourself, as he put it. I apologize for my boss's coarse thoughts."

Arnold stared at him, aghast. "You can't do this, I'm a surgeon – I'll never be able to work again if you do this." He could hardly breathe or speak – the dread and fear of what was about to happen overwhelmed him. He sucked in air as if he were asphyxiating.

"Ah, so that's it! Thank you Sir for giving me that information. It helps me understand my assignment. I don't like assignments that I don't understand. Our normal assignment is simply to terminate a target, but in your case we were told to make sure you don't die. Until now I couldn't figure out why we were only supposed to destroy your hands. Now I understand."

Slobber was running down Arnold's chin. "Please don't do this," he babbled.

"Of course I suppose that the pain and the dread of this moment could cause your heart to fail, but in that case I'm sure my superiors would understand, and would not hold your demise against my colleagues and me."

Arnold whimpered helplessly and stared at Bow Tie.

"Let me have it Gianni." Bow Tie held his hand toward the man.

The handler reached inside his jacket and withdrew a beat cop's nightstick and handed it to the little man. It was tightly wrapped in black, shiny leather. Bow Tie slapped it soundly into his palm, and appeared to be satisfied with its heft. He then turned back to Arnold.

"Sir please place your hands in front of you on the table."

Arnold didn't move. He couldn't. His arms were limp, not connected to his brain. He looked at the nightstick and began to sob. Mucous was running from his nose over his lips and down his chin.

"Sir, if you don't place them there yourself my colleagues will have to do it for you. I'm trying to give you an opportunity to have some dignity in this, to be a man."

Arnold couldn't raise his arms. The handlers looked at Bow Tie. He nodded.

The two big men each grabbed Arnold by a forearm and each placed a knee on his lap, one on either side. They stretched his arms out and held them flat on the table, palms down.

Arnold babbled; his lips and chin were covered with mucous and slobber.

"Sir, we'll be done here shortly and you can rest. Please bear with me."

Arnold watched as Bow Tie slowly raised the nightstick and then slammed it down hard. Light exploded in his brain and the sound was bones cracking and popping. He yelled. Bow Tie raised the stick again and slammed it down hard, and then he did it again, and again and again. The two brutes looked away, partly to avoid the splatter of fluids and partly because they didn't want to see the mess.

Arnold turned white but he did not completely faint. It took a few moments for his hands to bleed; he saw raw bone in the mangled mass at the end of his wrists; and he saw the dead hog hanging there and hog guts falling to the ground and Blair singing at church and Louise drinking old bourbon as she played her piano and the man lying there dead on the operating table.

Bow Tie stopped. He looked at his work and nodded. The handlers untied Arnold and helped him into a large stuffed chair. He was still semi-conscious. One of the men retrieved a towel from a bathroom. They placed the towel in his lap and his mangled hands on the towel. To finish the punishment, one of the handlers took a glass and a bottle of brandy from the liquor cabinet. He filled the glass with brandy and set it next to Arnold on the lamp table by his chair.

The whole process had taken less than ten minutes. They walked out the door and got into their car and drove off. They had one more assignment before leaving town. It was a quarter past six.

# AT THE SHERIFF'S PLACE
# AFTER CHICAGO

The men from New Jersey had watched the sheriff's work habits for several days. He arrived at his office at 6 o'clock every morning. Around 8 o'clock he walked over to Jack's Cafe and stayed there for thirty minutes to an hour and then returned to his office. He sometimes walked back over there around 10. He went to various places for his noon meal, and left the office at 3 o'clock and went home. He drove his patrol car into his driveway and turned around in the back yard so that his car was facing the street. Like most southerners he used the back door to go in and out of his house. Every evening he would leave his house at 7 o'clock and return to the office for a half hour or so.

The men drove from Arnold's house to Sam Bartlett's house and parked a half block down the street. It was almost dark. The streetlights were already on. At 6:55 Bow Tie knocked on the sheriff's front door and the handlers crept through the side yard and went to the back door. The back porch light was on. The sheriff came to the front door and turned the porch light on. Bow Tie apologized and asked him for directions to a motel that he couldn't find. The sheriff spoke to him and made several gestures pointing down the street. Bow Tie thanked him and walked back to the sidewalk. The sheriff went back inside. Bow Tie walked through the side yard to the back door.

At 7 o'clock the sheriff opened his back door and stepped outside. He awoke sitting at his kitchen table, tied to a chair, his wrists bound together with duct tape and stretched out on the table in front of him. What had been his hands was a tangled mass of flesh and bone. It would have been impossible for him to use his telephone or his radio. He couldn't connect his brain to his hands. He yelled. And yelled.

At 7:40 Burt Reedus turned into Sam Bartlett's driveway and nosed up to Sam's car. He heard Sam yelling for Billy Matson, faintly. He ran through the back door into the kitchen and stopped.

"Lord God Almighty! What happened? They got you too!"

The sheriff's pistol was on the table. A wet hand towel lay beside it. Burt pulled his pistol and quickly looked through the house. He came back to the table and lifted the towel to his nose. Chloroform.

"What happened Sheriff?"

Sam stared at his hands. He had spent his strength yelling and now could only whisper.

"I don't know. Seems like I remember some short slick haired little son of a bitch wearing a bow tie come to the front door asking directions. I talked to him and he left and that's the last thing I remember. We need to be looking for somebody wearing a bow tie."

Burt stared at the sheriff's mangled hands and felt sick. "I came over here to tell you Dr. Fulton's wife just called screaming that somebody'd busted his hands all to pieces. He's on the way to the hospital now. We were worried since you didn't show up at the office."

He dashed outside to his car and grabbed his mic. "Get somebody over here now!"

"Where?"

"The sheriff's house! Come on! He's bad off!"

"Ok. The rescue squad's on the way. Three minutes. You don't want to take him directly to the hospital?"

"I don't think I can drive. Just send'em!"

Burt set his mic back on its clip and turned away from

his car and vomited. He wiped his mouth and breathed heavily and deeply and went back into the house. He couldn't handle this. Sam had puked on himself. This was bad. He could smell Sam. He gagged. He rushed back outside and heaved until he heard the siren as the rescue squad ambulance rounded the corner. He couldn't go back inside.

The medics bolted from the ambulance as soon as it reached the driveway and ran toward Burt with their gurney. Burt nodded toward the back door and turned away from them. They left the gurney at the bottom of the steps and ran inside. The driver backed the ambulance down the driveway, stopped and went inside the house; after two or three minutes the medics came out supporting Sam between them. They eased Sam down onto the gurney and loaded him into the ambulance.

As they were sliding the gurney in, Burt stared at the sheriff, shocked. Clipped to Sam's collar right under his chin was a big black bow tie.

# THE INVESTIGATION

Since he was the chief deputy in the county, Burt was tasked with leading the investigation into the attacks on Dr. Fulton and the sheriff. The day after the attacks he talked to the Fultons' neighbors and to Jackson and his sister. He talked to Blair and asked her if she had any idea who would want to do something like that to Arnold. She laughed.

"Are you drunk?"

"No Ma'am."

"You must be. There's not a soul on this mountain that's not delighted about this. Would you care to join me for a drink?"

"No Ma'am."

When he was walking back to his car she yelled at him. "Here's something you can tell this whole mountain. I'm damn sure not going to be punished for this. If these people think I'm going to clean him up every time he goes to the toilet, they've got another think comin'! He's the one that hurt that little nigger – not me; so if you ever find out precisely who did us this favor I want you to give'em a message straight from me: You tell'em I said Thanks!"

She raised her glass of bourbon to Burt as in a toast, tipped it slightly toward him, and drank it down. Burt drove off. He wanted to talk with the sheriff's neighbors before lunch.

———

Burt talked to the neighbors across the street from the sheriff's house and to the neighbors on the other side of his house from Burnam's Store. Nobody had noticed anything. He talked to Mr. Burnam – nothing. As he was leaving he glanced at the chicken house behind Burnam's Store and remembered that Billy lived there. He saw Billy working in Burnam's garden and walked over and spoke with him.

"Yeah, I seen somethin', and it won't none of our people."

"How do ya know?"

"Cause I'uz in my house eatin' some supper and I heard the sheriff talking to somebody so I looked. The sheriff had his porch lights on and I seen a little man on the front porch wearin' a bow tie and while the sheriff was waivin' his arms up the street I seen two big men go around the house to the sheriff's back porch. Then I seen the sheriff go back inside and then the little fella went around back too. Ya cain't see the back door from my place, but I seen'em like they was going in the house and then a few minutes later I seen'em come out and walk up the street to a car, and the little slick-haired fella won't wearin' his bow tie no more."

"Do you know what kind of car it was?"

"Nope, but I know where it was from – by the time they left I'd gone out to the parkin' lot and when the car come by I seen the tag on it right under the street light."

"Where was it from?"

"New Jersey."

Burt knew the investigation had come to an end. They were long gone, never to be found. The car would have been stolen anyway. No sense in wasting any more time on this.

# THE GRIZZLED OLD
# WHITE DIRT FARMER

The grizzled old white dirt farmer sat at his kitchen table before daylight smoking his first cigarette and sipping on his first cup of coffee of the day, waiting for his woman to finish cooking breakfast. Thick smoked bacon sizzled in the frying pan, and its aroma mixed with that of the coffee invigorated him. He lived about half way down the mountain. He and his wife made a living growing cabbages and raising and selling a few more pigs than they needed for their personal use. He multiplied the value of these extra pigs by selling them not as live hogs but as cured and smoked hams, side meat, and sausage. Like many farmers on the mountain when he had something to sell he would take it to town on Saturday mornings. He would join the ad hoc farmers market by parking his pickup around the courthouse with other farmers and sell from the back of his truck. He never returned home with any of his cured pork. People gathered around his truck and bought his pork and cabbage almost as soon as he backed into a parking place.

He watched her remove the bacon from the pan and pile it onto a small serving plate, piece by piece. He sipped his coffee.

"I'm repentin'."

She broke four eggs into the pan and started scrambling them.

"Whatcha repentin' about?" she asked without turning.

"It ain't right the way we been treatin' our niggers all

these years. I ain't never done no lynchin' but I ain't been treatin' em right neither."

She stirred the eggs.

"Whatcha gonna do?"

"I don't know everything I'm gonna do, but I got some ideas."

"Ya reckon we oughta start by callin'em somethin' besides niggers?"

"Yeah, I reckon. I tried sayin' Negro when I'uz milking the cow while ago, but that don't sound right comin' outta my mouth. I believe I'm gonna start tryin' to call'em colored people."

"So how ya gonna do it?"

"Well, insteada sayin' that nigger that lives down there on the creek, I'm gonna try to say that colored man that lives down there on the creek."

"And what brought this on?" She refilled his cup.

"Well it just won't right for that little nigger girl to get her hand busted up like that. It just won't right. And then the way the judge handled the whole business it just kinda jerked a knot in my gut. I seen real pure righteousness – I mean real justice – when he done that."

"How ya know he's the one done it?"

"He done it."

She put the eggs and the bacon and the biscuits on the table. She sat down and looked at him. She had been looking at him and talking to him and listening to him every morning for sixty years. She had married him when she was fifteen and he was twenty, and she had given him his first son before she turned sixteen. They had buried two of their children and three of their grandchildren. She was seventy-five and he would be eighty-one next time. He still went to sleep with his leg draped over hers and with his old wrinkled bony hand on her chest. She knew this man.

"I reckon ya want me to repent with ya?"

"Yeah."

"Awright."

"We'll drive up the mountain here in a few minutes and take that best ham I got out there in the meat house to the judge. I heard folks are takin'im a little somethin' here and there to help'im fill his pantry. I been nursing that ham for three years for you an' me, but that's what I wanna do. I gotta start somewhere."

"Awright. I'll git ready."

# SANCTIFIED

**W**ithin two days, the whole mountain knew what had happened to Dr. Fulton and the sheriff. And then Mama started seeing what she said was the most amazing thing that she had ever seen happen on the mountain. For the next week, throughout each day leading up to Thanksgiving Day, cars and trucks and even mule-drawn wagons would pull up in front of our house and people would walk up to the front porch and leave a sack or a package on the swing or in one of the rocking chairs. They brought turnips, and ham, and fried chicken, and collard greens, and jars of pickles, and black-strap, and stuffed sausage, and little embroidered handker-chiefs, and a quilt, and a book, and nuts, and a couple of walk-ing sticks, and many other items from the mountain. Some-body even left some mountain nectar, that clear liquid that almost all of us came to appreciate after we passed into adult-hood. We were pretty sure it was three different people be-cause there were three different quarts of it, each delivered on a different day, and each having just the slightest difference in color, indicating that the offering had been aged in different wooden barrels for slightly different amounts of time. Mama spirited the first of the quart jars quickly into Daddy's study and asked him what he wanted to do about it, since it was clearly illegal. He thought for a moment and then he told her he would like for her to pour him a small glass and to store the rest of it in the liquor cabinet. He added that she was welcome to join him for a taste, and I was floored when she accepted. I had never seen her drink anything stronger than wine or beer. The two of them sat in Daddy's study facing each other and held small glasses. Daddy held his glass up and made a motion with it toward Mama, and she did the same and smiled at Daddy. He looked at her, raised his eyebrows, shook his head, and looked down at the floor; he then looked back up at Mama and motioned with his glass again and they drank. J. C. and I saw the whole thing.

The first few days it was mostly Cherokee people and black folks that brought things to the house. But then, white folks started coming up to the porch, placing items on the chairs and on the swing. It was the week of Thanksgiving and we were out of school. I had never seen people come to our house like this before. I was usually in the house and would look out the window when I heard a car drive up and a car door slam. Nobody knocked, and when more than one car or truck pulled up at the same time, nobody lingered and talked. They just brought packages up to the porch, set them down, and left, almost as if they were bringing gifts to the home of someone who had died.

Mama would join me at the window to look occasionally. But Daddy wouldn't come to the window and he wouldn't go to the porch to bring in the packages. Mama and I had to do that. Daddy had spent the past week holed up in his study reading and not talking much or out in the back yard messing with the pigs.

One of our town's citizens was a man named Thomas Langston. Tommy sold chewing gum on the streets in town for a nickel a pack. He had a fear of being touched by anyone so he would hand you the pack of gum by dropping it into your hand and then he would hold out his hand and you had to drop the nickel into it. He never went to the welfare office and it never occurred to anyone on the mountain to commit him to the insane asylum. He communicated only in monosyllables. Upon the completion of a transaction he would merely grunt and turn away. People said "He ain't right," and duly supported him by buying his chewing gum for thirty years. No one in town had ever seen Tommy touch another human being, but we all counted him as one of us.

Two days before Thanksgiving Tommy ambled up the walk to our porch.

"There's Tommy Langston!" yelled Mama. From her bedroom window upstairs she could see him coming up the walk. We were all surprised.

Tommy stepped onto the porch and walked up to the door, and instead of knocking he hollered "Com'ere!"

Mama ran downstairs and opened the front door.

"Hello Tommy!"

"I wanna talk to the judge."

"He's not available Tommy – he's just not feeling well today."

"I wanna talk to the judge."

"Tommy, I'm sorry but he really can't come to the door right now."

"Tell'im I said com'ere."

Mama was stunned. "He can't come out now Tommy."

"Tell'im I said come outchere right now."

Mama stared at Tommy with her mouth open, momentarily speechless, and then said, "Wait a minute."

Mama turned back into the house and a few moments later Daddy came to the door and stepped out onto the porch.

"Hello Tommy, how's it going?"

Tommy reached into his bag and pulled out a twelve-pack carton of chewing gum and extended it to Daddy with his left hand and dropped it into Daddy's left hand.

"Thank you Tommy."

Then Tommy reached out his right hand, fingers extended and palm down. He looked at Daddy's chest. Surprised, the judge looked at Tommy's hand; it was a fine hand, old, hairy, slightly trembling. Tommy looked at the judge's hand and just barely pushed his own hand toward the judge.

Slowly, unsure if he was doing what Tommy intended, the judge reached for Tommy's hand and took it in a skewed handshake, with the back of his own hand toward the porch floor. Tommy stared at the two clasped hands. With his left hand he reached up slowly and touched the judge's cheek, watching as his own flesh touched another. Mama shrieked. Suddenly Tommy let out a loud deep wailing sob, and then another and another as he looked at his hand in the judge's hand and squeezed it tightly.

The judge looked at the two hands holding each other and at Tommy's face contorted by the sobs, and at Tommy's hand still on his cheek, and he too started crying loudly; he pulled his hand from Tommy's hand and ran back into the house. Mama stood next to Tommy with tears running down her cheeks and openly weeping. Tommy turned and walked back to the sidewalk and ambled back toward downtown, looking at his hands all the way. Daddy paced around the house and then went outside and fiddled around in the back yard and the vegetable garden and the pigpen until dark. Several times I saw him wipe his face on his sleeve.

Two days later, on Thanksgiving Day, early in the morning, I saw an old Cherokee drive up in his pickup and just as he got out an old Negro lady hobbled up coming from the direction of Free Town, and then at about the same time a grizzled old white dirt farmer that lived down the mountain pulled up in his truck and got out. Each of them carried a package. The dirt farmer had his package cradled in his left arm and his old woman walked beside him on his right. It was a warm fall morning and our window was open. I stood at the window and watched and listened. They didn't talk to each other except when the old Negro woman stopped and motioned with her hand for the old white man and his woman to go ahead of her and follow the Cherokee up the walkway to our porch. She had done that for two hundred years, and for two hundred years the old white dirt farmer had stepped ahead of her. Now, he looked at her and then motioned with a toss of his head toward our house.

"Naw, go ahead."

She hesitated; she looked up at him and their eyes met and held for a moment. Then she nodded and stepped in front of him. The grizzled old white dirt farmer's woman slipped her hand into his.